Ghost of the Gunfighter

After serving twelve years for the accidental murder of a sheriff, the legendary gunfighter Tom Dix is released from prison. He is met by retired US Marshal Dan Shaw, the man who had brought him to justice. Shaw owes his life to the famed shootist and had grown to respect him. His intention is that he and Dix should ride north to Abilene to start a new life with their old friend James Butler Hickok or Wild Bill as he was known throughout the West.

But whilst Tom and Dan are on the way to Abilene, Wild Bill is in the midst of trouble. Despite ailing eyesight, the ageing lawman still strikes terror into the heart of badmen, many of whom have found their final resting places in Boot Hill. When the three finally meet up, Dix is but a ghost of the gunfighter he was but riding with Shaw and Hickok to restore law and order to Abilene, he proves he has lost none of his old skills and once again earns his place in the annals of legendary gunmen.

By the same author

Death on the Dixie

Ghost of the Gunfighter

WALT KEENE

A Black Horse Western

ROBERT HALE · LONDON

First published in Great Britain 2001

ISBN 0 7090 6883 2

Robert Hale Limited
Clerkenwell House
Clerkenwell Green
London EC1R 0HT

Typeset by
Derek Doyle & Associates, Liverpool.
Printed and bound in Great Britain by
Antony Rowe Limited, Wiltshire

Dedicated to Olive and Denis George

ONE

Barker was no longer a Louisiana town on the edge of civilization resisting inevitable respectability. That had arrived almost unnoticed many years earlier with the big brewers and the big manufacturers from back East. Now there were a mere ten saloons where once there had been over thirty. The gambling halls had been forced out across the wide Mississippi to larger towns with more transient populations.

Dan Shaw stood inside the marshal's office he had occupied for nearly six years and removed his badge for the final time. It no longer meant anything to the man who had spent his entire adult life upholding the law. Barker was simply no longer the same. It had been strange to see the town change from being a place where killings were an almost nightly ritual into a cosy niche where nothing happened unless it had to do with the faceless unholy factories. Factories which supplied the ever-growing West with everything it required.

Dan Shaw had grown to hate Barker as it had grown to pity him and his kind.

This was a day he had waited twelve long years for. A day which marked two very different things: his eventual retirement from a job which had become so boring it had sapped his will, and the release of Tom Dix from the Louisiana State Prison. Tom Dix was a man he had grown to regard as a friend during their short acquaintance.

Cupping the marshal's badge in his hand, Shaw thought about the monthly pension he was entitled to. It wasn't much to show for nineteen years of wearing various stars on his vests.

A deputy's star at first, which was replaced by a sheriff's and then he had become a United States Marshal. Yet with each change it seemed as if life in and around Barker had become less challenging. Where once he had risked his life to uphold the law using his wits and his guns, now it seemed his only duties were to serve scraps of legal papers from one large building to another equally large building.

Now that Barker had a small police-force based upon those back East, there was no place within its boundaries for reminders of a less sanitized time. Dan Shaw had become a constant reminder of those times.

He had to cut free.

For a widower not quite forty, it seemed that if he were ever going to find a place where he might fit in, it was not here amid the civilized folks. He had to go where men still were men and not merely cannon-fodder for factories. He had to find a place where men had not been trained to watch clocks.

Resting the shining badge on the ink-blotter Dan Shaw turned and walked out into the quiet street. He was now retired but felt as if this was the day when he would start living again.

He stepped down from the front of the building, gathered up the reins of his horse, put one foot in a stirrup and mounted the tall animal. Then he gathered up the reins to the other horse he had purchased and looped the leather around his saddle horn. It was a fine horse with a pretty good second-hand saddle and would suit its new owner just fine, he thought.

The ride through the quiet streets drew attentive eyes as usual. It seemed nobody rode horses in Barker any more. Only relics from a bygone age like Dan Shaw. Men who refused to accept times were changing. Refused to welcome so-called progress with open arms.

Men who spurned the loss of their freedom.

He knew they would not mourn his leaving here. These were not people like those who used to dwell in Barker. These were the civilized replacements who had brought their strange fashions and laws from another place. A place where men were nice and somehow not truly men at all.

Dan Shaw grinned to himself as he spurred the tall black gelding and began to make pace along the trail he had ridden so many times in the past. A trail which led to the ferry-crossing and the town of La Forge across the wide Mississippi. A place where men were still almost as bad as they had always been but also a town still a tad shy of what he was seeking.

As the small ferry began its slow crossing towards La Forge, Dan Shaw remembered the time when he had trailed the man who had killed Barker's town sheriff. How his blood had boiled as it flowed in his young veins that night.

It was the start of a journey which would alter his entire life and in a way change him from the boy he had been into the man he soon became. Tom Dix was the man he had tracked like the hunter he had once been in his youth, and yet was unlike anything he had envisaged or expected.

Stopping only to water the horses in La Forge, Dan Shaw rode past the large paddle-steamers and busy gambling-halls and countless saloons like someone heading toward paradise. He continued on through the sprawling town, full of people who still remembered how to have a good time, until he reached the trail that led east. La Forge still managed to keep the Bible-punchers and Eastern property-speculators at bay, but as he rode away from its distinctive noise and smell, he knew there was somewhere better.

With Tom Dix's help, he would find that place.

It was a long ride to where he was going and Shaw knew he had to arrive on time to greet the man he had not set eyes upon in over twelve years. The gates would open at precisely three o'clock to release the one-time gunslinger. Shaw would be there waiting.

Thundering along the leafy overgrown lanes towards the prison he began to realize why this part of Louisiana was so devoid of people. The aroma of the swamps filled the air here as he passed by mile after mile of lush greenery, heading towards his goal. No sane man would ride this way unless driven by a singular purpose, as Shaw was. There was a sweet-smelling decay all around the rider as he got closer and closer. Reaching a high hill that overlooked the prison, he reined up.

For what seemed an eternity, Shaw sat staring at the infamous place a mile or so before him. This was no place to live near, he thought. No man would choose to come within a hundred miles of this place. There was an evil atmosphere within that prison which seemed to fill the surrounding hills.

Maybe it was the combined souls of so many killers which made the horses skittish, Shaw thought as he spurred on. Perhaps it was the fact that the prison backed on to swamps which were filled with the devil's own creatures. Whatever it was behind the high walls that greeted the rider as he reached the gates, he knew he might never learn.

He had no desire to find out.

Dan Shaw sat atop his seventeen-hand black gelding, watching the imposing prison gates and wondering what horrors lay beyond them. What had the last twelve years done to the one-time gunslinger, Tom Dix? Shaw had encountered many men over the years and yet none could equal the sheer courage of the man who had willingly gone back with him, when he was a deputy, to stand trial for murder.

Dan Shaw recalled how he had trailed Dix after the gunslinger had accidentally killed his sheriff. How he had finally caught up with the gunslinger who was helping Wild Bill Hickok to catch a gang of cold-blooded killers.

He remembered how Dix had refused the false alibi which the famed Hickok was willing to swear to and admitted the truth to him.

It had been as if Tom Dix had actually been relieved when the then young Shaw had taken him back to stand trial. A trial which would have led to the gallows had it not been for the words which Shaw himself spoke on behalf of the quiet man.

Shaw knew Tom Dix had only been saved a death sentence because of his willing intervention, yet he wondered what effect twelve years in a chain-gang upon a man who had prized his freedom above all other things. Had he actually done him a favour or cursed him to something unimaginable?

A rope had been replaced by a sentence of a dozen years' hard labour which for some took an even greater toll. Many never returned through those gates. Many came back out to find themselves broken not only physically but mentally as well. Dan Shaw wondered how the man he had become proud to call friend, would handle the situation.

A score of requests to visit Dix had all been rejected by a system which had been designed to make the prisoners regret they had not been hanged.

What would Dix be like now?

Dan Shaw had brought a horse and fresh clothing for the man who had impressed him all those years ago. It was the least he could do for someone who he knew was haunted by that one stupid mistake in the shadows of a hotel lobby when he had pursued a killer and found himself gunning down the town sheriff. He had grown to learn that Tom Dix was no killer although he had lived by his gun skills prior to his fateful error.

As James Butler Hickok had put it all those years earlier, Tom Dix was a real man. A man of honour.

Someone whom you could trust with your very life.

Few men had ever impressed Wild Bill, but Dix had managed to do so without even trying.

Dan Shaw wondered to himself if justice had actually been served by sending such a person to prison. What might the man have achieved if he had remained free? In some part, Shaw had lived with a measure of guilt equal to Dix's own: Shaw's for not allowing the gunfighter to escape, Dix's for squeezing his triggers without first allowing himself to see his target.

Dix had been afraid that night so long ago. Fear had killed the sheriff as it had killed so many others before and after the event. It was a lesson Dix had learned to his cost. A lesson he had paid the price for.

As Dan Shaw pulled out his gold hunter watch from his vest pocket and opened its lid, he heard the sound he had waited nearly an hour for. The sound of the high, imposing prison gates being unbolted.

It was exactly three o'clock in the afternoon as the watch began to chime in his hand.

Looking up at the gates, the ex-marshal waited.

Then they began to be pulled open slowly.

The sight which met Dan Shaw's eyes horrified him.

TWO

It was a shambling figure who was pushed out through the open prison gates by the heavily armed guards. A man who was only just clinging to the very name itself by virtue of sheer determination and nothing else. His feet shuffled in ill-fitting boots as if unable to forget the shackles which had restrained his legs for over a dozen years. A grey beard hung over the shirt-front and hair protruded from beneath a Stetson which, like the clothes on his back, had long been a feast for a thousand generations of hungry moths.

The clothes hung on his lean pitiful frame as he shuffled forward, carrying a small bandanna holding his few possessions. He saw nothing as he walked aimlessly away from the prison gates as they closed solidly behind him. Only when the sound of the massive bolts filled his ears, did he pause and look back.

Suddenly the blank expression changed to one of horror as the pathetic figure realized he was now free.

There was no excitement on the man's face as he stood outside the prison, only the look of a confused creature who now had to find a life out here in the world of dark reality. Terror seemed to overwhelm the broken soul as he fell onto his knees and stared aimlessly at the soil around him.

Dan Shaw swallowed deeply as he quietly dismounted from the tall black horse and stood watching the shaking figure before him.

Could this be Tom Dix?

What had they done to him?

Fighting back his own emotion, Shaw moved closer to the kneeling figure who seemed unable to grasp where he was or what was happening to him.

'Dixie?' Shaw said in a hushed voice as he paused over the pathetic creature who seemed unable to stop shaking.

There was no acknowledgement of the words or of Shaw himself from the man who seemed afraid to look up at the ex-marshal. How many times had he been beaten for casting his eyes where they were not meant to stray?

'It's me, Dixie. Dan Shaw. Look at me.'

The face looked up at him with a terror forged

in the whips of countless thrashings behind the high prison walls.

Dan Shaw stepped closer to the man. He bent over to the almost unrecognizable face and studied it carefully. The hair was mostly white now and yet behind the wrinkled eyes he saw the spirit of Tom Dix still alive.

'It is you, Dixie. God, what they done to you?' Shaw asked as he found his hand touching the face.

'Dan?' Dix said as he focused on the face which, like his own, had aged since he had last set eyes upon it, so many years ago he had lost count.

Shaw gripped the upper arm and helped his friend back to his feet. He had never felt a grown man's arm so thin before and it chilled him.

'I brought you some new clothes and a new horse, Dixie.'

Tom Dix steadied himself on feet unused to the high-heeled boots which had waited over a decade for him to wear again and looked at the horse.

'I don't know if I can ride any more, Dan,' the sad voice said as he nervously edged closer to the handsome creature. 'I ain't even set eyes on a horse for so long. How long has it been?'

'Too damn long, Dixie. Too damn long.' Shaw choked back his emotions as he led his friend up to the horse and placed a hand upon its mane. 'I got you a real quiet one. He don't buck or nothing. I figured you would be a tad rusty after so long.'

Dix nodded. It was not the nod of a man agreeing with another but the obedient head movements of a man who had been punished many times for disagreeing with prison guards.

'He looks a nice quiet horse.' Dix looked into the large brown eye of the gentle creature.

'He's OK. I made sure of that for you. I'll help you up, if you want?' Shaw said as he saw a man whose spirit had been crushed long ago shaking beside him.

'I guess riding is easier than walking,' Dix said as he allowed the younger man to assist him in mounting the horse.

Dan Shaw handed the reins to Dix and tried to see if the face would change expression once he was seated in a saddle again. It stayed exactly the same. An equal mixture of terror and confusion.

Satisfying himself Dix was not about to fall off the horse, Dan Shaw put the small bandanna of possessions into the saddle-bag behind the cantle and moved around to his own horse and mounted quickly. He manoeuvred his black gelding alongside his friend.

'Why are you here, Dan?' Dix asked coyly, staring at his hands holding the unfamiliar reins.

'I come to help you.'

'Why?'

'Because we are friends, Dixie,' Shaw insisted. 'They ain't allowed me to visit with you in twelve years but we are still friends, ain't we?'

Tom Dix nodded. 'Yeah. We are friends.'

Shaw shrugged as he held on to the bridle of his friend's mount and slowly turned the pair of horses around on the overgrown trail until they were heading back in the direction he had come from.

'Enough questions, Dixie. I reckon we better go pay a visit to a barber-shop in La Forge.' Shaw tried not to look too hard at his friend's altered image.

Dix looked up at Shaw.

'A barber-shop? Hot water and soap?'

'Reckon you earned a little hot water and soap, partner,' Shaw answered, allowing the horses to walk slowly while he stayed close enough to steady his weary friend.

'Can I have a shave and a haircut too?'

Dan Shaw nodded as he gently urged his horse on.

'That seems like a darn good idea, Dixie. I reckon it would be nice to see what you look like without all that hair.'

Tom Dix said nothing as the two riders slowly made their way up the hill before them. Yet it was clear, by the wrinkles which etched his cheeks from his watery eyes, that he was smiling.

For the first time in a dozen years, Tom Dix was smiling.

Both riders arrived in the thriving La Forge late. It had been a slow ride from the remote prison to the colourful city set on the banks of the Mississippi delta.

Tom Dix was visibly nervous as he rode beside Dan Shaw into the brightly illuminated streets of the gambling mecca. It had been many years since he had seen so many people enjoying themselves. The sheer noise of so many like-minded souls made the frail rider feel overwhelmed.

Shaw recognized his partner's concern and kept closer to the trembling Dix as they rode deeper into the bustling heart of La Forge.

Noticing a bright barber-shop close to one of the smarter hotels, Shaw turned his horse up to the hitching rail and dismounted quickly before assisting his friend from his saddle.

Securing both their reins to the rail, Shaw took the saddle-bags off his friend's horse before leading Dix up on to the boardwalk. To his surprise Dix paused and looked down towards the nearby quay, where a magnificent paddle-steamer was berthed.

'Damn. I'd forgotten how pretty them river-boats are, Dan.'

'You'll get a better look at that boat later, Dixie,'

Dan Shaw told him, resting a hand upon his shoulder.

'How come?' Dix turned and looked into the face beside him.

'I got us a couple of tickets, that's why.'

Tom Dix allowed Shaw to lead him into the quiet barber-shop before speaking again.

'Why do we need to go on a riverboat?'

'Because it'll save us a heap of time getting to our destination, Dixie,' Shaw answered as he watched the barber moving towards them.

'Destination?' Dix asked.

'We are heading up to Abilene.'

Again Dix questioned. 'What we going there for, Dan?'

'Because according to the newspaper, that happens to be where James Butler Hickok is at the moment. He's the town marshal.'

Tom Dix began to smile as memories of the tall gambler returned to his tired mind.

'Wild Bill.'

'When you've cleaned up and put on the new clothes I bought you, we are heading up to that boat,' Dan Shaw said.

The barber stood before the two men.

'Yes, gents?'

Dan Shaw placed two silver dollars in the barber's hand.

'My friend here needs a hot bath and a shave

and a haircut. I expect you to please do your artistic best.'

The barber smiled broadly as he ushered Dix towards the rear of the establishment.

'Fear not. Your friend is the hands of a tonsorial genius.'

It took until nearly ten before the barber was satisfied with his handiwork. He brushed down the back of Tom Dix's new jacket and led him back to the waiting Shaw.

Shaw stood and nodded at the sight which met his tired eyes. Tom Dix had lost his excess hair and the offending beard and at least ten years. As Shaw rose to his feet he could at last recognize the man he had respected all those years ago when they were both much younger.

Dix now looked and smelled human again as he reluctantly approached Shaw.

'You look good, Dixie. Real good.'

'The clothes sure help, Dan. Thanks.' Dix seemed unable to take his eyes off the array of mirrors within the barber-shop as he tried to accept his own reflection.

Shaw stepped up to the barber and slipped another couple of silver dollars into the man's hands.

'You done a fine job, *amigo*. Much appreciated.'

The barber stepped closer to Shaw and whispered.

'What shall I do with his old clothes? They are not in very good condition.'

Shaw bent down toward the barber and spoke quietly.

'Burn them.'

The barber nodded as he watched the two men untying their horses and begin to walk them down towards the quay and the waiting white paddle-steamer, which was bathed in the light of a thousand coloured lanterns. Then, pulling out his pocket-watch from his silk vest, he checked the time before closing the door and locking it.

THREE

Abilene, Kansas, had been a thriving cattle-town only twelve months earlier, when the stock-pens of Joseph McCoy filled to overflowing with longhorns as they stood next to the Kansas Pacific rail-tracks. Then, as the railroads forged further west, allowing new cattle towns to establish themselves. Abilene went into a fast decline. The herds still arrived but now less frequently. Abilene had seen its bonanza come and go but even the few herds that travelled here seemed to evoke the wrath of its citizens.

Farmers in the outlying districts still objected furiously to the constant invasion of herds of longhorn cattle and the rowdy cowboys with their trail-drive pay, who had little to do once the herds were safely delivered into McCoy's stock-pens.

The town council had become more and more

hostile to the very thing which had allowed their unimportant town to become prosperous over the previous years. Tired of the hordes of cowboys who tore up the town whenever a cattle-drive reached the stockyards and the recent death of their town marshal, 'Bear River' Tom Smith, they voted to hire the one man whom they believed capable of taming the reckless drifting cow-punchers.

James Butler Hickok was not known as Wild Bill for nothing and they had heard he was the most feared of gunmen. He seemed to be the ideal sort to put fear into the riotous cowboys.

He had drifted into their town after travelling from one mining-camp and cow-town to the next since the end of the Civil War, seeking new victims of his mastery of the gaming-tables.

Knowing Hickok was in their vicinity the town council were not about to let him slip through their hands without offering him the well-paid position of town marshal.

Fame in the West was for some a fleeting acclaim. Yet it had seemed everyone knew of Wild Bill Hickok. He was a living legend due mainly to scores of dime novels based on his factual and fictitious exploits as a gunfighter. He had achieved further glory during the Civil War where he served as a Union scout along the Missouri border. During the war he had saved an entire

Union troop when he had ridden through the Confederate lines and brought reinforcements.

Wild Bill Hickok also had an insatiable appetite for the poker-tables, female company and drinking. This cast a shadow over the man who was famed for his telling of tall tales. Yet it seemed no matter how many errors of judgement the flamboyant character found himself making, his extraordinary charm and total ability to convey his lethal prowess won over all doubters.

Whatever else the famous James Butler Hickok was, he remained one of the sharpest shots ever to enter Abilene. This alone kept his critics at bay.

He was their town marshal and had been unanimously voted into the position by men who were not about to change their minds in a hurry.

The sound of a rooster greeting the new day had interrupted the all-night poker game within the stale-smelling Red Garter Saloon. Yet somehow the five remaining players had continued for another two hours whilst the awesome figure of James Butler Hickok continued to stare from beneath his wide hat-brim at the quartet who had taken most of his stake money.

'Fast Hands' Doyle was an Irishman who talked continually to himself as well as the other players and was seated to Hickok's right. A slant-eyed man of dubious origins sat directly across the table from the town marshal and never said anything as he had played and won most of the pots.

There were two very different characters seated to the left of Hickok. The furthest away was a man called Don McKay. He was a prosperous owner of three stores in the sprawling town and had everything the visiting cowboy could want, for a price. A very high price. Anything from spurs to women, as long as the cowboy paid cash.

The card-player closest to Hickok was a larger man who growled most of the time and stroked his pile of chips continuously as he played. His name was reputedly Foster Holmes and he had only been in the cattle-town for a few days.

Hickok stared down at the meagre stack of chips before him and then at the cards in his left hand. For eight hours he had seen the stack diminishing steadily as he watched the original eight players filter down to the four around him.

At first he had imagined it was just not his lucky night until he spotted something happening between the remaining players. Signals drifted back and forth between the men as the players grew more and more confident that the tired marshal was getting sleepy or too drunk to notice.

Hickok's naturally heavy-lidded eyes did not have to do much to give the impression of weariness when in actuality, he was still wide awake. If he slept at all, it was usually during the afternoon, which was the habit of most professional gamblers.

Men like the flamboyant Wild Bill seemed to attract the card-sharps to him whenever he sat down at a poker-table. He accepted it most of the time but as he listened to the wall clock chiming ten in the otherwise empty saloon, he became angry. These men had set out to beat him at poker. To Wild Bill Hickok, this was the ultimate insult.

Licking his lips beneath the heavy moustache he began to realize how these men had set him up. They had known he could not resist the temptation of a big game and when he had sat down the previous night with his three hundred dollars, he had played himself into their well-oiled trap.

Studying his hand of five cards for the umpteenth time he sucked in air and then rested the five cards face down on the green baize before pulling out a long cigar from an inside pocket of his long frock-coat.

He bit off its tip and spat it on to the floor, where a dozen of his previous smokes had ended their life, then the blank-faced gambler placed the cigar between his teeth.

'What's wrong, Bill?' McKay asked from behind his cards as he watched Hickok striking a match and raising it to the end of the cigar.

'You boys are good, I'll say that.' Hickok's words drifted on the smoke which left his mouth before hanging over the circular table.

For a moment, the men all laughed. Then they began to notice the face of the marshal. It was cold like steel.

'You hinting at something?' Doyle queried.

'Wild Bill ain't saying nothing, Fast Hands,' McKay interrupted the anxious player.

Hickok leaned back in his chair until it hovered on its back legs and stared down the length of his cigar at the assembled gathering. The grips of his two pearl-handled pistols jutted grimly at them from beneath his jacket. They had all heard tales of the man who was supposedly the master of the cross-draw and as he brought both his hands up and cupped them behind his neck, through his mane of long hair, they began to wonder if those stories were indeed true.

'I don't like the looks of this, McKay,' Foster Holmes said. He felt the sweat trickling down his face as Hickok rocked on his chair beside him.

'Easy, Holmes. Bill is just having his fun,' McKay said as he too began to sweat.

'I ain't joshing, McKay,' Hickok said through the smoke which marked his every word in the stale saloon air.

'Guess it's time we called it a night,' McKay suggested as he began to rise from his chair. 'Reckon we ought to cash up and head for home.'

'You ain't going nowhere,' Hickok told them.

The four men all began to shift nervously in their chairs as the tall thin man placed the heel of his left boot on the edge of the table to steady himself.

'What do you mean, Bill?' McKay asked again as he placed his cards on the table and produced a handkerchief to wipe his face.

'You telling us we gotta stay?' Doyle asked angrily.

'Yep.' Hickok nodded.

The silent man with the slanted eyes looked at the other players. At last he spoke clearly enough for each and every one of the players to understand.

'I told you this was a mistake. I told you it was too damn dangerous to try and steal a pot from under the nose of Wild Bill Hickok.'

'Shut up, you fool,' Holmes snapped angrily, throwing his cards at the frightened man.

Hickok laughed at the ceiling.

'I knew it. I knew you boys had set me up.'

'We never set you up, Hickok. You just ain't much of a poker-player nowadays,' Holmes commented dryly.

'Our friend with the strange complexion and oriental eyes says different, Holmes,' Hickok said slowly glancing at the flustered man to his left.

'He's loco,' Holmes protested.

'I say you're a pack of lowdown dirty cheats,'

Hickok drawled in his most fearful of voices.

McKay leaned across the table toward the marshal.

'Just a little joke, Bill. We was having ourselves a little joke, that's all.'

Hickok turned his head slightly to look at the face.

'It ain't funny, McKay. I've killed men for less.'

Foster Holmes pushed his chair backward with his feet and rose to his full height. He was a big man but that mattered little to Hickok. He had killed far bigger prey in his time.

'You all thought you would take me to the cleaners?' Hickok asked the four men.

'I'm going and I'm taking my winnings with me, Hickok,' Holmes announced as he reached for the pile of cash stacked neatly on the edge of the table.

Hickok shook his head slowly back and forth as he pulled his hands back from behind his head and held on to his coat lapels.

'Nobody is leaving here just yet, Holmes. Especially you. Sit down.'

'I will not sit down, I'm going to my hotel room!' Holmes shouted down at the awesome creature who puffed on his cigar.

Faster than the blink of an eye, Hickok kicked the legs from beneath the man standing before him. Foster Holmes fell heavily into the sawdust between McKay and the town marshal.

For a moment, the startled man said nothing. Then as he realized his dignity as well as his back-bone had been bruised, he began to scream a long line of venomous words at the still-rocking town marshal.

'You quit cursing now?' Hickok asked as the embarrassed gambler paused for breath.

The room suddenly went silent as the big man rolled on to his knees and glared at the narrow-eyed marshal.

'What do you figure on doing, Hickok?' Holmes asked as he began to rise from the floor, covered in sawdust.

Wild Bill Hickok stopped rocking on his chair and stood up swiftly. Resting his thumbs in his belt he stared through the smoke of his cigar at the rising gambler.

'Let's give the pot to Bill?' McKay suggested.

Doyle shrugged and then reluctantly nodded as he tossed his cards on to the pile of coloured wooden chips. The man with strange slanted eyes nodded frantically at the suggestion.

Only Foster Holmes seemed either unwilling or unable to accept that they should hand over the money to the marshal.

'I say no.'

Hickok stood with his pistol-grips pointing at the figure who was now facing him. A man who had pushed his coat-tail over the handle of his Remington.

'You don't want to give me the pot, Holmes?'

'Nope.' Holmes sucked in air and squared up to the marshal.

Hickok nodded as he looked down at the three seated card-players.

'You three men can go. Me and Holmes have something to discuss.'

McKay, Doyle and the strange-looking man did not require telling twice. They all rose quickly and fled the saloon before the ash had fallen from Hickok's cigar. As the saloon doors swung back and forth, the elegant marshal concentrated on the defiant figure before him.

Still Foster Holmes seemed unwilling to back away from the notorious gunfighting legend.

'It's just you and me now, Hickok.'

'Was it your idea to try and cheat me?'

'Sure was. Them lame brains ain't exactly bursting with an abundance of guts.' Holmes allowed a wry smile to etch his features as he faced his target.

'That your real name, Holmes?' Hickok asked as he removed the cigar from his lips and placed it on the table.

'You are a little brighter than I imagined, Hickok.'

'What they call you really?'

'Does it matter?'

'Not really. I just like to know what to tell the undertaker when he's having your tombstone carved, that's all.' Hickok tried to figure where he had seen the face before him. It had not struck him when the poker game had started in the gloomy lamplight but now as the sun penetrated the saloon windows, Hickok knew he had seen images of this face before.

'You wanted?' Hickok asked as he edged closer to the man.

'Reckon there ain't no harm in telling you now we are alone. I'm wanted dead or alive.' Holmes laughed.

'That's a damn shame,' Wild Bill Hickok said under his breath. He watched his opponent's fingers beginning to twitch.

'How come?'

'Now I've got to kill you.' Hickok raised both his hands and watched the man opposite him do the same. 'I ain't one for cluttering up cells with prisoners when a wooden box will do the same job.'

Holmes's eyes flashed at the wall clock as its minute-hand drew closer to the quarter-hour.

'When the clock chimes, we draw.'

'Agreed,' Hickock said coldly.

There was a long pause before the clock finally chimed the quarter-hour. Within a split second of the noise reaching their ears both men seemed to go for their weapons at exactly the same moment. A blinding array of flashes lit up the interior of the saloon as exploding hot lead burst from their guns. It seemed as if the sound of the bullets bounced off the wooden saloon-walls for minutes after the men had ceased squeezing their triggers.

As the choking gunsmoke began to clear, James Butler Hickok stared down at the body before him. Holstering his guns he stepped over the lifeless form and leaned on the table.

'Wish he'd told me his real name,' Hickok muttered to himself as he began picking up the money from the table. 'I've got to look through a pile of Wanted posters now until I find out who he was and how much he's worth.'

FOUR

Tom Dix had found it impossible to sleep the previous night aboard the massive paddle-steamer. As soon as the first hint of dawn had shown itself through the cabin window, he had risen, dressed and left his sleeping partner to roam the quiet decks. Standing on the top deck of the riverboat surrounded by luxuriance he had never imagined possible, he simply stared blankly out at the shoreline as the *Delta Queen* moved ever on through the vast waterway. The determined progress toward Brinkman Point, where they would disembark and continue their journey on horseback never faltered. Hour after hour the riverboat ploughed through the dark water aiming for its first port of call, Boone's Landing. Yet none of this meant anything to the troubled Tom Dix.

He had had so many dreams as vivid as all this so many times over the past dozen years, only to find himself still shackled like an animal when he finally awoke.

Was this just one more cruel flight of fancy in a mind which had been tortured beyond most beings' imagination?

It seemed very real, Dix thought.

That meant nothing. He had once imagined he was in a flower-filled meadow when in reality he was lying face down in other prisoners' filth. He could not trust any of his senses any longer. They had betrayed him so many times.

Walking slowly beside the rail until he reached a point high above the massive red water-wheel which drove the huge boat through the water, Dix wondered what was happening to him. The smell of the water filled his nostrils and took him back to a time when he was much younger and far more confident.

The one-time gunfighter who had been quite a card-player in his prime rested his elbows on the damp rail and looked at the white foam trailing away from the stern of the big vessel.

What was he doing here?

Was he really here at all?

Had he been released or had his mind finally broken under the twelve years of misery he had endured?

Recurring questions that seemed to come into his mind every few minutes. Questions he could not answer.

Dan Shaw had said they were heading to Abilene to meet up with James Butler Hickok.

Although he wanted to see his old friend again, he wondered whether the feeling would be mutual.

Then he recalled the carnage he and Hickok had found themselves embroiled in all those years ago aboard another paddle-steamer. How he and the living legend had ridden together and fought side by side.

Would Hickok even remember him?

The most chilling of the thoughts that continually drifted into the mind of Tom Dix was a simple one; was this all a bizarre dream?

Was he really standing upon the deck of the *Delta Queen* or was he still back in the Louisiana State Prison shackled to a rotting bunk waiting to be awoken?

He had spent twelve years having such dreams. Dreams which had become nightmares as soon as he had opened his eyes to find himself still there amid the filth.

Without knowing why he began to shake again as if unable to control the overwhelming fear that rose inside him.

Was this real?

Truly real?

'I've been looking for you, Dixie,' the familiar voice said from behind him.

Tom Dix turned and looked at the smiling face of Dan Shaw as the man approached.

'I couldn't sleep, Dan,' Dix heard himself explain.

Shaw rested his elbows on the rail beside the troubled man and looked out at the view they were leaving behind them.

'You OK?'

Dix shook his head. 'I'm going crazy, Dan.'

'Figured as much,' Shaw said.

'You did?'

'Can't be easy to come out of that hell hole and suddenly find yourself free again.' Dan Shaw sighed.

'I ain't sure that I am free, Dan. This could be just another cruel dream.' Dix choked on the words.

'It's real.'

'I can't be sure of that. For all I know I've lost my mind and am imagining everything. Even you might be nothing more than a dream, Dan.' Tom Dix rubbed his hands together as if unable to relax for even a brief second. It was the fear of a man who was terrorized by his own inability to free his mind from the shackles that had chained his body for so long.

'I reckon in your place I'd feel exactly the same.' Shaw cast a fleeting glance at his new partner. 'It'll take time.'

'I'm scared to shut my eyes and go to sleep in case when I open them again, I'll be back there.' Tom Dix turned away from the water and leaned his back against the railings. He stared up at the twin black stacks as they billowed out black smoke.

'You checked the horses?' Dan Shaw tried to change the subject briefly.

Dix nodded. 'They're fine up in the forward stables, Dan.'

'Did they seem real?'

'I guess they did, Dan.'

'Come down to the cabin with me and go to bed, Dixie. I'll sit next to you until you wake up.' Dan Shaw's voice had a strength in it which the older man trusted. 'You need rest and good food to wash away them demons, partner.'

'I'm scared, Dan,' Tom Dix admitted bluntly.

'You got the right to be scared, Dixie,' Shaw said. He pulled himself away from the rail, gripped his friend's arm and began leading him towards the stairwell. 'The thing is though, I ain't going to let them nightmares come back.'

The pair walked down the cast-iron steps and along the shaded walkway until they reached their cabin. Shaw unlocked the door and let Tom

Dix enter before following him in. Then he closed the door behind them, opened the drapes and allowed the daylight to enter the pristine room.

'Take off them boots and get some shut-eye,' Shaw instructed the nervous Dix who reluctantly complied.

'Is that an order?' Dix smiled as he fluffed up the soft pillows.

'Yep.' Shaw nodded. 'That's an order.'

As Dix crawled on to the soft bunk and inhaled the smell of fresh linen he fell instantly asleep.

Dan Shaw sat on his own bunk and watched his friend. At the first sign of Dix having a nightmare, he would wake him, he thought.

FIVE

It was late afternoon when Tom Dix opened his eyes and lay on his bunk staring around the cabin. Dan had lit the wall-mounted oil-lamp as darkness had begun to envelop the room. As Dix rubbed the sleep from his eyes he saw his friend sitting and watching him.

'You ever been told you snore something awful?' the retired marshal asked as he lowered his legs over the side of his bunk and looked at Dix thoughtfully.

Dix rose to a sitting position.

'Folks have made the odd comment to that effect, Dan.'

Shaw put his feet onto the floor before stretching. He moved to the table, lifted the water-jug and poured two glasses before returning with them. Dix accepted one and drank its contents in one go.

'Hungry?' Dan Shaw asked as he drained his own tumbler.

'Sure. I could use some food now, partner.'

As Dan turned to replace the empty drinking vessels on the table he sighed heavily to himself. At last it looked as if Tom Dix was beginning to break free of the past, he thought.

'Get them boots back on and let's go find us some vittles. I think we deserve us a couple of thick juicy steaks.'

As the two men left their cabin and began heading along the deck in search of a dining-hall, it seemed to Shaw that his friend had grown an inch or two during his slumbers.

It was obvious to the two men that the *Delta Queen* was far from full on this trip. The dining-room had only served two other customers during their long meal and as they strolled into the large adjacent gambling-hall it seemed as if only forty or so people were seated within its elegant setting.

'Drink, Dixie?' Shaw asked his companion as they strolled through the array of empty tables toward the long brass-railed bar.

Dix raised an eyebrow. He had not had any liquor for so long he no longer desired it.

'I don't really feel like drinking, Dan.'

Shaw raised a hand to one of the bartenders when they reached the highly polished surface.

'You sure? What about a beer?'

'OK. I'll have a beer.' Dix nodded, then caught sight of his own reflection in the long mirror behind the well-stocked bar.

'You look pretty good.' Shaw grinned as he saw his friend studying his own image in the mirror.

'I sure look old,' Dix said.

'You are old, Dixie. We're both old.' Shaw grinned when the bartender reached them. 'A whiskey and a beer, please.'

'Coming right up,' the man said.

'What the hell are we doing on this tub, Dan?' asked Dixie.

'Heading on up to Abilene, partner,' Shaw replied. He placed a coin on the bar and accepted their two drinks. 'I figured it would take weeks of hard riding for us to get there on horseback but if we booked passage on the *Delta Queen* as far as Brinkman Point, we'd only have a few days' riding from there to Abilene.'

Dix sucked in the beer suds and suddenly found himself smiling as he began to remember how good beer could taste.

'Are you rich? This must have cost you a lot of money. My new horse and the gear and this trip and all.'

Dan Shaw sipped at the whiskey.

'I had me a house. I sold it. Remember our share of the reward money we earned with Wild

Bill all them years ago? I put it in the bank where it remained for twelve years.'

'Reward money?' Dix had forgotten all about their share of the money they had earned for recovering the steam-boat company's funds. 'I figured that all went on the trial.'

Dan laughed. 'I let the county pay for the trial. I figured if them lawyers knew you had money they'd just take it all off you and still manage to lose the case. Lawyers are like that.'

'I thought I was broke,' Dix gasped. 'You mean I got me a few dollars?'

'More than a few. I put all the reward money in an account and let it make interest for us, Dixie,' Dan Shaw beamed. 'It made us a lot of interest over the years.'

Tom Dix watched as his friend reached into his inside coat-pocket and produced a wallet which he then gave to him.

'What's this?' Dix asked as he looked hard at the soft leather in his hand.

'Your share. Interest and all,' Dan said. He finished his drink and raised a finger to the bartender for a refill.

'How much is here?' Dix asked, staring at the heavy leather wallet in his hand.

'Nearly four thousand dollars, Dixie.' Dan watched the startled reaction of his partner. He seemed to be weighing the heavy wallet in his hand as if he were a human set of scales.

Dix raised an eyebrow again.

'That's an awful lot of money. Are you sure this is all mine and you ain't made a mistake?'

'I've got a lot more than that. Remember, I had me a house to sell.' Dan Shaw grinned as he picked up his whiskey and took a sip. 'We'll need every penny if we're going to start a new life out West, Dixie.'

'Before I went to prison, all I was any good at was using my guns, Dan. Sticking with my sort ain't healthy,' Dix said.

'We're partners from here on in,' Shaw insisted.

Dix followed the man away from the quiet bar to an empty card-table close to the roulette wheel which was doing the best business in the large rooms.

'You must be the most honest *hombre* I've ever met, Dan.'

'Takes one to know one, Dixie,' Shaw said as he watched the bargirls emerging from behind the stage curtain and beginning to mix with the mainly masculine clientele.

Dix placed the wallet in his inside coat-pocket before taking another swallow of the beer.

'I've got something else of yours in my bags in the cabin, Dixie,' Dan told his friend.

'What?'

'Your guns,' Shaw said over the rim of his thimble-glass as he sipped at the whiskey.

Tom Dix lowered his head.

'Them guns cost me a dozen years of my life, Dan.'

'They also saved the life of James Butler Hickok and yours truly, Dixie,' Dan told him.

SIX

Word travelled fast from one town to the next concerning the news of the death, in a deadly duel, of the outlaw Foster Holmes at the hands of the famous Wild Bill Hickok. Maybe it was the railroad which linked them that sent the chilling information along its steel tracks, or perhaps it was the daily stage and its gossiping passengers.

However it journeyed, within half a day of the event it seemed as if everyone within a two-hundred-mile radius of Abilene had heard how Wild Bill had yet again snuffed the flame from another bandit's candle.

The story varied as it passed from one eager teller to the next and by the time word reached the quiet rooming-house in Silver Springs, fifty miles north of Abilene, it had managed to develop into almost epic proportions.

By the time the afternoon single-sheet newspaper was handed out freely to the guests in small rooming-houses, Hickok had managed to slay an entire gang led by Holmes.

The three men who had rented room and board for the past week read the information with a mixture of emotions. To them, the news that was printed on the hastily published paper held something personal.

The three men were no mere travelling salesmen, as they had registered, but were in fact members of Holmes's gang. They had gathered there, waiting for their leader to telegraph them to join him in Abilene.

Everything had been carefully planned down to the smallest detail by the man who hid behind the pseudonym of Foster Holmes in order to disguise his true identity.

Now their plans had been dealt a hefty body-blow, which none of the outlaws had anticipated, and none would accept.

The meanest of the trio was a well-dressed man who had been known by many names over his long career as an outlaw. This day he answered to the handle of Black.

'So Tulsa got himself killed by that no good Hickok.'

'The paper might be wrong. Maybe there was another dude using the name Foster Holmes,

Black.' The second man, who was named Grainger, suggested to his two companions as they brooded in the parlour of the rooming-house.

The third man was equally well attired. He was known as McQueen. He shook his head and faced the lace drapes.

'Ain't much chance of there being two men with that handle, Grainger. I agree with Black, Tulsa is dead.'

For a few minutes none of the three outlaws spoke as they allowed the shocking information to sink into their devious brains.

Then Black rested his hip on the side of a padded chair. He curled his index finger and drew his partners closer so they could hear his subdued tones as he spoke.

'The plan will still work even without Tulsa. We was only waiting for him to set the ground for us to arrive. Renting a couple of rooms and the like. We can still pull this off, boys.'

McQueen rubbed his fine suit-leg as he tried to be as positive as his growling companion.

'The plan had not taken Hickok into consideration, Black.'

Grainger nodded. 'Tulsa never said Wild Bill Hickok was the town marshal in Abilene. I don't want to go up against him when he's in form.'

Black shook his head.

'Tulsa never said nothing about Hickok because

he never knew the fancy pants was there. That's why he got himself plugged, I figure.'

McQueen nodded.

'Black's got a point, Grainger. Tulsa must have been spotted by Hickok. Maybe it was just bad luck.'

'That's what I reckon, boys. Just bad luck.'

'You could be right,' Grainger conceded.

'Then all we got to do is take the evening stage to Abilene and keep our noses clean until we get things organized.' Black was grinning in a fashion unique to himself.

McQueen looked hard at Grainger.

'I say we catch the night stage like Black suggested. We would be fools to throw away this chance.'

'I guess I'm with you boys, but Wild Bill still frightens me.'

'You ever had your picture took?' Black asked the more cautious member of his band.

'Nope.'

'What about you, McQueen?'

'Nope, I never had my picture took,' McQueen answered. 'Why?'

'No pictures means no faces on Wanted posters, boys.' Black smiled even wider than before.

'So Hickok won't even suspect we are wanted.' McQueen began to show his teeth.

'Exactly.' Black stood and smashed his fist into

the palm of his hand. 'That was Tulsa's weakness. Vanity. He had his picture took in every damn town we ever visited. That's how they got his face on the Wanted poster. That's how Hickok must have recognized him, by the pictures.'

The three men headed toward the small desk.

'We're checking out, pilgrim,' Black informed the owner of the rooming-house. 'What do we owe you?'

James Butler Hickok had spent far too many evenings looking at the world through the bottom of an empty whiskey glass. It had became far more of a habit during the past few months than ever before he knew it. Yet it seemed no matter how much he drank the true power of the liquor never affected him in the way it did normal men.

There had been a dry spell up until he had drifted into Abilene; then he had fallen back into his old ways.

Unlike most drunks though, Hickok knew why he was drinking more and more as time drifted on.

He had a reason.

A damn good reason.

Since the end of the Civil War he had been troubled by a recurring eye problem. At first he had thought it was the just effects of too many all-night poker-games and rot-gut whiskey, but then, even when he had gone months without touching a drop of alcohol, it persisted; he knew the problem was serious.

For most people the slow loss of one's visual abilities holds no fear as it is chalked down to age, but when you have lived by your skills as a gunfighter and poker-player, the thought of possible blindness offers nothing but stark terror.

So far, Hickok had managed to bluff his way out of any possible trouble when the affliction had come over him. So far, nobody had noticed.

Perhaps it was the naturally hooded eyes and fixed expression, the epitome of the 'poker face', which had managed to save his neck from the young guns who would relish drawing on him when he was temporarily unable to focus.

Maybe it was just pure luck.

Wild Bill had been blessed with an abundance of luck all his life and even now, as the sight in both eyes drifted from honed perfection to blurred mists, it stayed with him.

He had killed two cavalrymen in Hays City a short while before coming to Abilene. He had been the law and his charm had managed to get him cleared of any wrong-doing, as usual, but he knew the real truth.

They had started something whilst he was having an attack and the mocking which had dogged him all his days caused him to draw and kill the men outright.

The one fact he did not tell anyone during the hearing was that he had not seen either trooper before drawing his weapons and letting loose with their deadly venom.

At that moment he had been quite blind.

Only a score of years had saved him that day. He had heard the men slapping leather and simply used his instincts to aim in their general direction.

No one had been more shocked than Hickok himself that day when he was told that he had gunned down two cavalrymen. The blindness had lasted several hours that day. Hours when all he could see was the blurred shimmering of outlines and colours.

Yet he had managed to bluff his way out of any wrong-doing because they had started it. The local papers had reported he was drunk because he had staggered away from the scene of carnage but he had not been drunk that day.

Hickok had staggered because he simply could not see the obstacles that had got in his way as he had desperately sought his office.

That was the day when he had started drinking heavily again to try and blot out the terror being unable to see brought him. Yet he could not get drunk. He had never been able to get drunk.

Sitting in the cold hotel-room he finished the

bottle, placed it on the dresser near the window and stared down into the street now aglow with street-lights.

There had been so many towns over the past couple of years, he thought. It had been as if he had visited them all as he drifted aimlessly, haunted by a reputation which had always managed to get there before him.

James Butler Hickok watched the people milling around the town seeking and finding a good time. Tonight his eyesight was as good as it had ever been. He could see as well as when he had been a young buck in short pants. Every detail was noted by the tall slender town marshal as he lifted his hat from the back of the wooden chair next to his bed and moved to the door, only pausing to check his reflection in the long mirror before leaving the room.

Walking along the landing towards the impressive flight of steps that led into the busy lobby held no mysteries for Wild Bill Hickok.

Not this night. Tonight the citizens of Abilene would not risk making him angry. A fresh killing always had that effect.

As he made his way through the crowd of mumbling people out on to the boardwalk of the street he maintained his image to all who beheld him.

Pausing upon the wooden walkway he lit a

cigar and inhaled the strong smoke deeply into his lungs. They were talking about the man he had gunned down in yet another duel which would go down in history, if he had half a chance of retelling it.

Studying the long street and the dozens of dark corners he wondered how long it would be before his eyes let him down once again.

Would the next time be permanent?

He ran a slim finger along his moustache, gritted his teeth and tried to think of something less morbid. He had still not checked his huge pile of inherited Wanted posters to find out exactly who Holmes actually had been. But that could wait.

Right now he felt lucky.

It seemed to the man who had become a legend long ago and had been forced into trying to live up to the hundreds of tall stories that had been written about him that his very existence now hung in the balance. No matter how many times he tried to shrug off the thought, it kept returning to him.

Suddenly losing the ability to focus on a hand of cards was annoying but not likely to get you killed.

Losing the ability to see when someone was calling you out to an old-fashioned gunfight was another matter all together. If that happened, there would be nothing even Wild Bill Hickok could do.

When it had happened in Hays City, he had been lucky. It happened on a quiet street where at least he could hear his foolish opponents. In a noisy saloon or gambling hall, there would be nothing he could do.

He had plugged the wrong person more than once due to his eye trouble.

How long had he left before somebody put two and two together and wrote about it in the local newspapers? Then the story would be picked up by papers further afield and they would come looking for him.

All the back-shooting vermin who shied away from Hickok – the legendary gunfighter – would come seeking him if they even suspected he was losing his sight.

Hickok knew there were hundreds of outlaws who would happily like to add his notch to their gun-grips.

Hickok puffed on the long cigar and stared down the busy boardwalk. Folks still tipped their hats at him or gave him a wide berth knowing his reputation, knowing that the man in the fancy clothes wearing boots which went nearly up to his crotch was no man to mess with.

This was a man with quicksilver for blood. His mood could change as quickly as the weather in these parts. Hickok still evoked fear in all who were intelligent enough to recognize his prowess.

The afternoon sleep had made him feel confident again. The quarter-pint of whiskey had also helped.

Stepping down from the boardwalk, Hickok headed for the brick building called the Gamblers' Den.

Whatever was brewing in the complicated mind of the tall slender man as he strode towards the building, he looked as if he felt lucky.

It was an immaculate illusion.

SEVEN

The Overland Stage routes had been whittled down to a mere memory of their former glory since the railroad had forged through Kansas, securing its links with the Eastern cities. It was only the places where the trains did not go that still kept the company going. At one time, before the railhead was established in Abilene, there had been six stages a day passing through, on their way from one place to another. Now there were a mere three stages a week, and even these seemed to be eventually doomed.

That was what the educated called progress. Others had far more colourful words to describe it.

As the six-horse team pulled the dust-caked stagecoach to a halt outside the run-down offices just after two in the morning, it did not get a second look from any of the cattle-town's nocturnal population.

Its three neatly dressed passengers stepped from the coach and onto the lantern-lit boardwalk. They proceeded to brush the dust from their clothing whilst they waited for their luggage to be thrown down from the roof of the stage by the shotgun guard.

Black, Grainger and McQueen said nothing as they strolled along the still-busy street carrying their hand luggage. Black led the trio as usual in a precise manner. His were eyes that saw and remembered everything which might prove useful at a later date.

Grainger followed Black and was in turn trailed by McQueen down past the array of busy saloons and gambling parlours. They moved like men who knew their business.

They did. They knew it inside out.

That's why they were still alive whilst so many others in their trade rested in various cemeteries.

Although they had lost Tulsa, and he usually planned their jobs with immaculate detail, it was the three remaining members of the gang who always carried out the dirty work. As they walked in silent procession along the streets of Abilene they already knew every aspect of this dare-devil caper. Tulsa had spent weeks putting every part of the operation into place and they had rehearsed their roles to perfection, like actors in a play waiting for first night.

It would have been helpful if the mastermind had not allowed Wild Bill Hickok to kill him, but these were professional men who adapted well. They had lost men before and it had become nothing more than a minor annoyance.

Now, in Abilene, they would rehearse the final act before doing the deed. They would check to see if everything was where Tulsa had said it was. No detail would be overlooked or ignored. They knew the price of failure; it was called death.

One by one the men walked into the busy lobby of the grand red-brick Taverstock Hotel and moved to the main desk. It was an impressive building by any standards and reflected the influx of Eastern money.

Black leaned on the desk and tapped the small gleaming bell as his partners joined him at either side. All three looked the epitome of respectability as they waited for the hotel night-clerk to appear from behind an expensive-looking velvet drape.

He was a small man somewhere in his sixties with gold-rimmed glasses perched upon the end of his nose.

'Yes?'

'We are looking for some rooms,' Black said in his most educated of voices.

'Three rooms?' The small man stared at them

as if unable to make up his mind about something they were not aware of.

'Yes, three rooms if possible. Adjoining each other,' Black continued. 'My friends are in Abilene on business and we like to stay close to one another.'

The man began to make a tutting noise as he flicked through the pages of the thick register before him.

'Three adjoining rooms? No, no, no. I simply cannot manage three rooms adjoining, sir. Out of the question.'

Black listened for a few seconds as the tutting continued from the small man's mouth before interrupting.

'Do you have two rooms adjoining?'

'Two rooms?' The man turned and squinted at the array of keys hanging behind him and seemed to be doing some sort of mental arithmetic as he pointed his thin index finger at each key in turn before returning his attention to Black and his silent companions. 'I can give you room 45 and 46 on the top floor. Will that do?'

'Does one of the rooms have two cots?'

'Oh yes. They both have two cots apiece and indoor plumbing just down the hall.' The small man smirked.

'Sounds good.' Black pulled out his thick wallet and unfolded the tight wad of bills within its leather belly. 'How much for the week?'

The man pulled a small pencil from his vest pocket and licked the tip before jotting down a series of numbers on a scrap of paper next to the register. Looking up, he spoke.

'Twenty-six dollars and fifty-eight cents.'

Black peeled three ten-dollar bills and dropped them into the man's hands. 'Keep the change.'

The man began to raise both eyebrows as he calculated how much his tip was. Then a smile etched his little face, as he realized this was his first tip since he had taken the job of night-clerk at the hotel.

'Thank you kindly, gentlemen.'

Black signed the register for himself and his comrades as the two keys were handed over.

'Thank you, my friend.'

'A pleasure, er, Mr Black.' The man nodded as he read the name off the page before him. 'Is there anything you require sent to your room? Drink? Or perhaps something of a feminine nature?'

All three men smiled at once.

'Not tonight, it's a little late.' Black grinned.

'Of course. What about food?'

Black led his men towards the wide carpeted stairs.

'Two plates of sandwiches and a pot of coffee will do just fine,' he said over his shoulder. He led McQueen and Grainger to the first landing, where they aimed their dusty boots in the direction of the next, less impressive, flight of steps.

The little man beamed as he thought about getting more tips from these neatly dressed men.

'I shall see to it personally, Mr Black.'

EIGHT

It had taken only five days to reach the muddy shores of the place known as Brinkman Point since Tom Dix and Dan Shaw had embarked. Five days of smooth water had seen the two men with very different backgrounds set their sights on the long ride to Abilene which lay ahead. Little had happened of any note as the two men got to know each other again after so many years. With Dan Shaw's encouragement Dix had finally begun to accept the fact of his freedom. An excursion around Boone's Landing had enabled the one-time gunfighters to purchase some trail gear.

Now it was time to leave the riverboat and begin riding the lonely, hazardous route which would eventually take the pair to Kansas and the notorious cattle-town of Abilene.

Both men were filled with a mixture of emotions as they pondered what lay ahead of them. This was a trail known for its ruthless ambushes. Since the end of the Civil War countless scores of men lay in wait along the densely overgrown roads. These were men who had grown accustomed to the killing they had once been required to do, and were somehow unable or unwilling to stop their merciless ways and return home to a more sterile life. The scars of war still hung over the Southern states like a festering wound which refused to heal.

If nothing else, imprisonment had at least spared Tom Dix from becoming one of the war's many victims.

The massive *Delta Queen* paddle-steamer dominated the tiny quay which marked the beginnings of the shambling town on the edge of the Mississippi. Never a place of any great note to those who visited and certainly a disappointment to the wretches who lived within its boundaries, Brinkman Point had little to offer those who sought something to write home about but it had one thing going for it, a natural landing ideal for the huge riverboats which traded in goods rather than passengers this far north.

Dan Shaw led his magnificent black gelding down the wooden gangway carefully as his friend Tom Dix followed with his own mount. Both men were now dressed for the trail in heavy hard-wearing clothes and were sporting leather chaps around their legs to protect them from the sweat of their horses.

Shaw still wore his pistols in the same holsters upon the same belt that he had worn for twenty-odd years but Dix had not yet strapped his guns back on.

Tom Dix still remembered how his guns had killed an innocent man and how that had robbed him of twelve years of his life. It was a memory which remained just beneath his skin like an itch it was impossible to scratch.

'You gonna put your guns on now, Dixie?' Dan asked.

Dixie shrugged. 'When I'm ready.'

'It can get dangerous in these parts for a man who ain't armed,' Dan warned.

'How dangerous?' Dix asked as he remembered all the places he had drifted through when he was younger and how his gun skills had saved his bacon on more than one occasion.

'There are those along these trails who will skin an unarmed man alive just to get the fillings out of his teeth, let alone steal the horse from beneath his butt,' Dan said bluntly as he opened the flap of a saddle-bag, pulled out a gunbelt and held it out to his partner.

Dix took the belt from Shaw and reluctantly strapped it around his hips before checking the well-maintained pistols.

'Did you clean my rig, Dan?'

'Every month for twelve years.' Dan smiled.

'I don't like wearing them any more.'

'If there is trouble on the trail, we have a chance if you're wearing them guns. I ain't never been much of a shot,' Dan admitted as they began walking again.

The ground was always sticky with black mud around the quay as the waters of the great river lapped constantly at its shoreline, threatening to flood the township one day when the time was right.

The two men moved through the crowd of workers who descended upon the boat like locusts on ripe crops, until they reached dry ground.

Dan Shaw stared around the grubby array of buildings which made up Brinkman Point before grabbing hold of his saddle horn and hoisting himself aboard the tall black mount.

'I reckon we got us a good ride before we hit the Kansas plains, Dixie,' he said.

Dix carefully raised his left boot until it fitted neatly into his stirrup, then he pulled himself up onto his saddle. He sat looking across at his pal before speaking.

'I feel kinda heavy.'

'You ought to feel heavy, you've eaten some fine vittles over the past few days.' Shaw grinned as he pulled his mount alongside the older rider. 'I figure them steaks have put a bit of flesh back on your pitiful frame, Dixie.'

Dix nodded. 'Any towns between here and Abilene?'

'Yep. A heck of a lot of towns. Why?'

'I don't cotton much to trail grub, Dan,' Dix said honestly as he tapped his spurs into the horse as he watched his friend leading the way.

Dan Shaw looked over his shoulder as he teased his reins against the black gelding's neck. 'I heard tell there's a small inn about fifteen miles up the trail, Dixie. If we ride hard we might get there before dusk. We could stay there tonight if you prefer?'

Dix nodded again. 'I surely do prefer.'

'I ain't cooked a meal on the trail for years, Dixie,' Dan sighed thoughtfully.

'You forget that I've tasted your cooking before, all them years ago when you took me back to Barker, Dan. I ain't hankering to taste it again if there's a choice.'

'Since my wife passed away, I've become quite good with a skillet, Dixie,' Shaw informed.

'Even so . . .'

As the two riders reached the edge of the town and headed along the dark overgrown trail it seemed to them both as if they were heading out on a journey they should have started many years earlier.

Neither rider spoke as they allowed their mounts to find their own pace.

Abilene remained its rowdy self as the three well-dressed men walked out from the hotel and studied the surrounding buildings for the umpteenth time. It was early afternoon and the sun was hot as it blazed down on the crowded streets. There was a smell in the air which had not been there before, the smell of a huge herd being loaded into the vast stock-pens down near the rail tracks.

Black turned to his two associates and grinned.

'At last, the big herd has arrived.'

McQueen bit the end off a short thick cigar and placed it between his teeth before striking a match down the wooden porch upright. Cupping the flame he drew in the smoke before allowing it to drift back out through his teeth.

'I was beginning to think old Tulsa had made a mistake.'

'Me too,' Grainger agreed running a finger around his stiff collar. 'We've been here for three days. I was getting edgy.'

'You're always edgy, Grainger,' Black said as he stepped down into the street and wove his way through the passing horsemen in the direction of the railhead.

The two men followed him closely as he led them through the small alleys they had discovered during their enforced stay in Abilene.

'I knew Tulsa wouldn't let us down. His plans are always on the money,' Black said. He marched into an adjoining street and stepped up on a boardwalk before continuing in the direction of the unmistakable aroma.

'He got the date wrong,' McQueen puffed.

'He was close enough,' Black snapped, forging ahead of his companions. 'It ain't easy to give an exact date when five thousand head of steers are going to reach a place like Abilene, boys. He was only a few days out.'

'That is pretty good, I guess.' Grainger panted as he worked hard keeping up with the two fitter men.

Then Black stopped and rested his knuckles onto his hips. He was staring at the dozen or more cowboys as they herded the cattle through the choking dust into the awaiting pens which seemed to go on as far as the eye could see through the shimmering heat haze.

'Look at that, boys.' Black sighed.

'Impressive.' Grainger coughed as the smell of five thousand steers overwhelmed them.

McQueen sucked on his cigar as he narrowed his eyes against the dust. 'I hate cattle.'

Black raise both his arms and rested them around his two associates' shoulders.

'Smell it?'

'Sure do.' Grainger sniffed.

'What do you smell?'

'I smell cattle,' Grainger replied.

'That ain't what I smell,' McQueen puffed.

'Money, boys. That's the smell of money.' Black began laughing as he squeezed the shoulders of his partners. 'Them steers are the key to our fortune, boys. Just like Tulsa planned. I can smell the money already.'

McQueen shook his head and turned away. 'Your nose must work different to mine, Black. All I can smell is a bunch of stinking cattle.'

'After them steers are sold off, we strike.' Black smiled.

'How long will that take?' Grainger asked as he followed Black.

'Two days at the most, I figure,' came the confident reply.

NINE

They had covered nearly ten miles since leaving Brinkman Point along barely visible trails that wove through dense woodland on all sides. The almost tropical vines which hung from unkempt branches like snakes waiting to ensnare anyone foolish enough to travel this way had slowed their progress. It seemed as if green was the only colour here where bushes as high as three-storey buildings loomed to both sides of the trail. It was obvious that Dix and Shaw were the first riders to venture down this dirt-track for many a long while.

Rounding yet another twisting bend at a mere canter, Dix reined his horse to a halt; his partner stopped his tall black gelding next to him. Only the most ambitious of rays from the blocked-out sun managed to penetrate the green canopy and filter into the gloom before them.

Dix stood in his stirrups for a second and concentrated at what lay ahead. His face seemed troubled.

'What's wrong?' Dan Shaw asked his partner.

'Thought I saw something,' Dix replied as he steadied his anxious horse.

'You sure?' Dan Shaw had to fight with his frustrated black gelding as they hovered on the slight rise in what could have been described as a clearing compared to the dark mystery which faced them.

'Nope. I ain't sure but this horse is.' Dix ran a hand over the snorting head of his mount. 'He's sensed something and it's made him a tad concerned.'

'Could be a lion or maybe a bear,' Shaw suggested.

'Or men,' Dix added as he glanced across into the troubled face of Dan.

Shaw bit his lip and stared into the darkness of the overgrown road. He could not see a thing but that did not mean there was nothing there.

'What you figure we ought to do, Dixie?' he asked.

Dix rubbed his chin. 'We ain't got a lot of options, Dan. We either quit and head back to Brinkman Point or we carry on. If you got a third choice, I'd sure like to hear it.'

'Something caught your eye, huh?' Dan soothed

the neck of his black gelding and continued staring into the gloom ahead of them.

'I could have been wrong but as we rounded the bend back there I thought I caught a glimpse of a man dashing across the trail.' Dix pointed. 'This gelding spooked too. Must have been something moving.'

'Could be them army renegades I heard tell about.' Shaw could feel the sweat running down his spine beneath his shirt as he spoke.

Dix inhaled deeply, flicking the safety loop off his right-hand pistol before withdrawing it from the holster slowly and cocking its hammer.

'If I was going to try and dry-gulch someone, that would be the perfect spot, where the trail gets real narrow.' Dix spat wrapping the loose reins around his left hand until he had raised his mount's snorting head.

Dan Shaw swallowed hard watching his friend.

'So we're heading on?'

'Reckon so,' Dix answered slowly as he continued trying to see into the darkness ahead of them.

Dan drew one of his own guns and nervously pulled its hammer back with his thumb, emulating his partner.

'What's the plan, Dixie?'

'We ride hard and fast straight down that trail,' Tom Dix said in a voice somehow devoid of any hint of fear. 'If we're lucky and I was wrong, we might just survive. It could have been just a trick of the light.'

'What if it is them renegades, Dixie?'

'Then we got ourselves a fight on our hands.' Dix sighed heavily. 'Are you ready?'

Shaw nodded, pulled his horse next to Dix's waiting for the older man to give the word to start. He did not have to wait long.

Tom Dix gripped his reins in his left hand tightly as he raised himself in his stirrups holding the cocked gun in his free right hand. Using his entire body like a human whip, Dix somehow managed to get the horse beneath him to charge forward with his partner at his side into the darkness.

The two riders thundered side by side along the trail, then, suddenly, saw a rope being raised to neck height across their path. As the two men hauled at their reins, trying frantically to stop their horses riding into the vibrating obstacle in front of them, they heard the excited screams coming from both sides. Screams which were quickly followed by the sound of gunfire.

Without a second's hesitation, Dix leapt from his horse and dragged Dan from his saddle to stand beside him. Bullets flew over the heads of their horses as their attackers made sure they did not hit the two mounts. Tom Dix and Dan Shaw stayed between the two terrified animals as they heard the gunfire all about them. It was clear to Dix that there were men on both sides of the narrow trail.

Grabbing at his pal's shoulder Dix ducked beneath the tall black gelding before making for the thick undergrowth. With every step, Dix held his pistol at arm's length and fired in the direction of the bushwhackers. Although well hidden in the dark green bushes, the black smoke from their discharging rifles and handguns gave Dix more than a hint as to where they were.

Hauling Shaw down on to the ground, Dix quickly drew his other gun as his eyes desperately sought out a glimpse of their adversaries. Shooting into the smoke seemed to be his only choice and it proved a good one.

Blasting away with both his weapons in steady fashion, Dix heard the first of his shots finding its hidden target. Then another scream was followed by a man falling out of the bushes and landing on the trail as blood squirted from his fatal wounds.

Shaw held on to his guns and began firing blindly as the true magnitude of their plight dawned on him. In twenty years of upholding the law in and around the town of Barker he had never found himself in anything as bloody as this.

'Steady, Dan. Don't waste bullets,' Dix said. He trained his weaponry on the end of the rope stretched tight across the trail and fired. Suddenly the rope went slack as a man fell out from the cover of the bushes and rolled limply on to the trail. The firing continued and the two men watched as their horses raced off down the trail.

'The horses,' Dan Shaw shouted in alarm as he watched the terrified animals disappearing out of view.

'Don't worry about the horses.' Dix pulled his friend down as bullets tore up the tree directly behind where they were kneeling.

Shaw lay on his side as he watched Tom Dix expertly empty the spent shells from his pistols and reload them from the bullets in his gunbelt. The entire operation was completed in less than sixty seconds by hands which had not forgotten something they had learned so very long ago.

Dix pulled Shaw's arm and they moved speedily through the bushes as men seemed to appear from their hiding places and head for where they had just been. Dix picked off one as they were moving and knew his shot had been deadly accurate by the way the man fell.

Once again it was Dix who pulled his partner down behind the trunk of a huge tree as he stared through the swaying leaves at their opponents who were now coming at them from two sides.

Rising to the side of a stout tree, Dix began to pull his gun-hammers back with his thumbs. His fingers squeezed the triggers of the two lethal Colts.

The bushwhackers crouched as they closed in on the pair, making it difficult to see them, let alone hit them. A volley of Winchester bullets ripped through the dense bushes beside Dix before he managed to move. Then bullets came from another direction and forced him to duck down. The crossfire continued until Dix managed to see and shoot one of the approaching men.

Shaw seemed numb as he knelt where Dix had placed him. He held both guns but seemed unable to understand the situation which they had ridden into.

Then Dix rose again and began firing faster than seemed possible to the open-mouthed ex-lawman. Every shot found its target until there seemed to be only a few of the stunned vermin left.

Dix felt his gun-hammers fall on to empty chambers once again, and he holstered both his pistols before grabbing the weapons from his partner's hands. Even as bullets began to rip apart their new hiding-place, Dix stood against the tree and continued firing until there were no men left standing.

For more than a minute, Dix stood beside the tree holding the guns in readiness, waiting for yet another attacker to show himself. It proved a vain wait.

He had finished each and every one of them.

As the choking cloud of gunsmoke finally began to drift away from the horrific scene, Dix bowed his head and lowered the weapons silently.

Dan Shaw was shaking beside Dix's leg as his guns were handed back to him.

'Load them, Dan,' Dix said as he pulled his own guns out of his holsters and allowed the hot shell-casings to fall from their chambers.

'Ain't it over?' Dan asked fumbling with his guns, trying to do as he had been instructed.

'It's over all right,' Dix said. He slid his loaded Colts back into the holsters and sighed heavily. 'But empty guns ain't much use in these parts, are they? I heard tell there are bushwhackers around here.'

Dan rose to his feet and followed Dix out of the thick brush back up on to the trail. The two men stared at the bodies all about them. Fourteen bodies dressed in what used to be uniforms lay where they had fallen. Each had been killed with such deadly accuracy that it beggared belief.

'Damn,' Tom Dix said as he began walking in the direction their two horses had fled only minutes earlier.

'I never seen such shooting, Dixie,' Dan Shaw said as he walked beside the brooding man. 'I was scared but you just faced them *hombres* and fought.'

'I was scared too, Dan. I ain't ever been so damn scared.'

Dan continued to keep pace with the grim-faced Dix. 'You OK? You ain't wounded are you?'

'I ain't even scratched.'

'Thank God.'

Dix shook his head; his eyes could not help but stare at his deadly handiwork. 'I don't think the Lord would approve of any of this, Dan.'

'But you ain't done nothing wrong, Dixie. They was out to kill us and you bettered them.' Shaw rested a hand on Dix's shoulder.

Dix screwed up his eyes and stared ahead. 'How far do you reckon the horses have gone?'

'Not too far, I hope,' Shaw replied.

'How far are we from Abilene?' Dix kicked at the dirt beneath his feet.

'Maybe less than a week's ride, I reckon. If we catch the horses, that is,' Dan Shaw answered. He realized that Tom Dix did not wish to dwell on what had just occurred, only on what lay ahead.

TEN

Three days had passed by almost unnoticed by everyone within Abilene since the massive cattle herd had arrived, except by the three neatly attired men. For all that time the steers had waited in the hundreds of swollen stock-pens alongside the railtracks, waiting to be shipped back East. However, for that to happen, the buyers' agents had to arrive before the auction could take place. It mattered little to most of the parties involved apart from the three men led by the one called Black.

For Black, Grainger and McQueen this was something they had not anticipated. Something their dead comrade Tulsa had not added to his sophisticated plans. They had been in Abilene now for six days. It felt as if they had spent an eternity in the town as most of their time had been taken up trying to avoid the hooded eyes of the one man they all feared, Hickok.

They knew there was no way the famous Wild Bill could identify them from the vague descriptions upon their Wanted posters, but he was smart. They had ventured out only after sundown each day and tried to stay away from the places he was well known to frequent. They had spent six long dry hot days in the two rooms they had rented on the third floor of the Taverstock Hotel. At this time of year it seemed to remain hot even during the hours of darkness, and they knew it.

'Going out for your nightly constitutional, gentlemen?' the desk-clerk asked as Black led Grainger and McQueen down into the hotel lobby.

Black ambled across to the small, elderly man and smiled as he rested his elbows upon the wooden surface.

'Any news about the cattle auction?'

'I did hear a rumour around the Drover's Rest Saloon that the last of the cattle agents was arriving tonight on the midnight train, Mr Black.' The clerk smiled as he adjusted the gold-rimmed glasses on his nose.

Black began to grin. 'So that would mean the auction should be tomorrow?'

'Around noon, I imagine,' the clerk confirmed.

Black pulled out a silver half-dollar and placed it in the little man's hand.

'Many thanks, my friend. That's exactly the news my associates and I have been waiting for.'

'You going to bid?'

Black shrugged as he headed towards the large open doorway with his men at his heels.

'Something like that. Something like that.'

'Where we headed?' Grainger asked as they walked out into the relative darkness of the lantern-lit street.

'I figure we better check out this Drover's Rest Saloon, boys,' Black said as he marched along the boardwalk towards the noisier part of town. The part where the cowboys were still celebrating the end of their trail drive in the only way they knew how.

'How come these cowboys ain't lit out of town by now, Black?' McQueen asked as he trailed behind Black.

'They ain't been fully paid off yet. Only after the sale of the herd will they get the rest of their wages,' Black answered. His legs forged on towards the sign he had memorized, like all the others around Abilene.

The three men walked into the Drover's Rest Saloon in single file, looking for cowboys still sober enough to answer a few questions.

Through the dusty window James Butler Hickok surveyed the scene of rowdy cowboys shooting up the town outside his office with more than a little interest. This was why the Abilene town council had employed him, to stop the mayhem the trail hands caused after being paid off following a long trail drive. For the most part these were youngsters who rode up and down the dimly illuminated streets shooting their guns wildly at anything that caught their fancy. He rose from his chair, where he had been ploughing through a two-foot-high pile of Wanted posters, lifted his long frock-coat from its peg and slipped it on.

He checked his pearl-handled revolvers before holstering them, then he opened the office door and stepped out on to the dark boardwalk.

Standing for a moment like a magnificent statue, Hickok tried to gauge the situation before acting. Running his fingers through his mane of hair, he began walking along the wooden boardwalk in the direction of the saloons and gambling-halls. There were at least a half-dozen brothels dotted in various secluded side-streets and he knew every one of them. As he strode on his long thin legs he pondered the situation carefully. The days when he would simply head straight into the heart of trouble were far behind him. Now he had begun to use his wits.

Pausing on the corner of Main Street he leaned against a wooden upright, pulled out his silver cigar-case and withdrew one of his favourite smokes. Biting off its tip and spitting it at the ground, he placed it between his teeth.

The long match burst into flame as he ran his thumbnail across its red tip. He sucked in the smoke several times before blowing at the match and discarding its blackened twisted form.

The sounds of cowboys having a good time echoed around the large town. This was a new experience for the famed lawman. He had never before been in a town when such a massive herd had arrived. He could understand why these young men were doing what they were doing but it was his job to make them do it quietly, if at all possible.

As two young riders came tearing around the corner from the seemingly endless stockyards, and headed towards him, Hickok stepped down from the boardwalk and paced slowly to the centre of the wide street.

Facing the approaching cowboys as they raced towards him, firing their guns wildly, Hickok drew both his pistols and cocked their hammers.

As the pair of young hotheads bore down on the tall figure standing in the middle of the street they began firing at him as if he would react the way everybody else did when faced with guns spitting lethal lead.

That was their first mistake.

Wild Bill Hickok stood as the bullets ripped up

the ground around him without even blinking.

Raising his pistols as the riders got within fifty feet of him, Hickok squeezed both triggers.

Even in the darkness of the long wide street Hickok's bullets found their targets. Both men felt their guns being torn from their hands as his bullets found their mark. Reining to a stop, both of the young cowboys dismounted drunkenly and ran at the tall unemotional figure. When they got within a few yards of Hickok they saw his guns glinting in the light from a nearby store-front. Then as they stopped, they began to study the figure who loomed above them.

Without uttering a word, Hickok pulled the hammers back on both his guns again until they locked into position.

'Wait a dang minute here,' one of the cowboys slurred as he pointed at the stone-faced marshal.

'What is it, Tate?' the second cowboy asked as he too tried to take in the frightening sight before them.

'I know who this dude is.'

Hickok stood glaring at the pair without speaking. The two men cautiously approached.

'Is you Wild Bill Hickok?' The first cowboy began to hiccup.

'I heard of him. Is that him?' The other cowboy stopped and began to rub his face as he tried to focus on the man who had two gleaming pistols trained upon them. 'Reckon we ought to go someplace.'

The first cowboy took another defiant step forward and rested his hands on his hips.

'You don't scare me. I'm from Texas, Hickok.'

Hickok lowered one of his guns and fired. The bullet ripped through the leather of the cowboy's holster, severing it from the belt.

'I don't like cowboys,' Hickok announced. 'In fact I usually kill anyone who even admits to being a cowboy. I ain't partial to Texans either. You being both, I reckon I ought to kill you right now.'

The second cowboy grabbed his stunned friend and dragged him back.

'We better go someplace and get some shuteye. This is Wild Bill Hickok and he don't like our sort.'

The cowboy stared down at his ruined gunbelt before pulling away from his pal and began to turn.

'You don't frighten me, you long-haired bastard,' the cowboy shouted.

Without saying anything Hickok squeezed the trigger of his left-hand gun and sent a bullet through the cowboy's loose pants into his buttocks. Blood squirted out from the neat wound. The youngster squealed in agony as he realized he was bleeding from his rear.

'He's shot me in my butt.'

'I'm going. I'm going,' the second cowboy shouted with his hands in the air.

Hickok began to walk towards the pair. 'Take your horses and get the hell out of here. You annoy me.'

The two young cowboys staggered back to their skittish horses and led them hurriedly down an alley as the marshal stooped to pick up their guns from the ground.

As the tall flamboyant figure began moving deeper into the heart of the troubled town he tossed both the cowboys' weapons into an overflowing water-trough. It was going to be a long night, he thought to himself.

From the shadows of a nearby saloon three well-dressed men watched as Hickok strolled past them. He did not give them a second look as he walked deliberately down the centre of the street. Women of a certain profession smiled as he passed by them. He touched his brow to each and every one of them as he proceeded onward down the middle of the dark street. Many had heard the shots and stayed glued to the boardwalks as the man with the grips of his pearl-handled pistols jutting out from his lean middle, made his way slowly in the direction of the noise ahead.

As cowboys saw Hickok, they all seemed to retreat into the safety of the large saloons.

Black rubbed his chin as he watched Hickok step up on to the boardwalk, push his way through the swing-doors, and enter the crowded Drover's Rest Saloon. As soon as the tall town marshal had entered the brilliantly illuminated drinking-hole, it went silent.

'No wonder Tulsa's dead,' Black whispered to his two companions.

'I ain't never seen a man like Hickok,' Grainger admitted as he felt the sweat running freely down his temple. 'He must have ice for blood.'

'He sure cuts a mighty fine figure,' Black gulped.

'At least we found out that the cattle auction is tomorrow, Black,' McQueen said, as his eyes trailed the faces of his two companions.

Black nodded. 'Yeah, after all them steers have been sold, we can do the job we came here to do and then get out of here.'

ELEVEN

The sky was filled with a million stars as Tom Dix tossed the last of the kindling on to the blazing camp-fire. Somewhere out on the almost flat land around them a solitary coyote howled at the half moon. It was a chilling sound. Dan Shaw scraped the debris from their two tin plates into the flames and then rubbed sand over them before sliding them back into his saddle-bags.

'I hope that critter ain't hungry, Dixie.'

'Coyotes don't usually bother folks,' Dix said, remembering his days as a drifter.

Shaw moved to the camp-fire and sat down on his open blanket as the howling continued chilling his bones. 'You sure about that, Dixie?'

'Yep, but cougars can be a bother.' The older man laid his head on his saddle and tucked his Stetson under his neck.

'You're starting to make me nervous,' Dan said, staring out into the darkness as sparks from their fire floated across the otherwise silent plain.

'How far are we from Abilene now, Dan?' Dix asked. 'My bones can't take many more nights lying on hard ground out in the middle of nowhere.'

'I figure we're really close, Dixie,' Dan answered. He pulled off his boots and laid them next to the camp-fire's white-hot embers. 'How long have we been riding since we last saw another human face?'

'Two or three days. I've lost count.' Dix sighed as he felt his bones beginning to relax. 'I must be crazy to have agreed to make this trip.'

'Once we get to Abilene we can have us a grand old time with Wild Bill. It'll be like old times.' Dan pulled the blanket over his shoulders and lay facing the fire as he wondered about their strange journey. A journey filled with bloodshed.

'By the time we get there Wild Bill should have retired of old age.' Dix sighed as he stared up at the black sky.

'We might get there tomorrow if we're lucky. I ain't too sure though.' Dan Shaw rubbed his chin as he thought of how the feeble creature he had witnessed leaving the prison had somehow changed into something resembling his former self.

'You better be right because I don't think my guts can take another of them home-cooked meals,' Dix muttered.

'My cooking ain't that bad, Dixie,' Shaw protested.

'Sure.' Dix rested his hands on the grips of his guns and closed his eyes. The sound of howling coyotes had never bothered him; they reassured him he was still alive.

Twenty miles away James Butler Hickok was leaving the High Hat Gambling Hall with the last of the young cowboys under his arm. Blood from the deep gash on the crown of the cowboy's head traced their route out into the street.

Dropping the helpless wretch at the feet of a couple of older, calmer trail hands, Hickok gave his last command of the long night.

'Get this young buck to a hotel room and bed him down.'

The two drovers nodded, dragged the limp youngster off the ground and carted him away.

As the long-legged town marshal mounted yet another boardwalk he paused by the swing doors of a saloon just long enough for him to check his pocket-watch in its light.

It was nearly five in the morning and he was unusually tired considering he had not taken a drink all night long. The town now seemed to be far quieter than when he had left his office just after sunset the previous evening.

He had taught the rowdy cowboys a lesson they would not forget quickly. At last the members of the town council might get off his back long enough for him to play a little poker and visit a few of the more friendly of Abilene's female population.

But not tonight he thought, as he strolled back into Main Street. Tonight he had earned his salary the hard way and was in no condition to cooncentrate on either cards or women. Just as he was about to head in the direction of his hotel, he began to think about the man who had called himself Foster Holmes.

It was as if his mind had cleared and the face of the dead card-sharp suddenly filled his thoughts.

Turning on his heels, Hickok strode down the street in the direction of his office with renewed vigour. He turned the brass handle, pushed the unlocked door inwards and entered his office. He moved to his cluttered desk where the stack of Wanted posters lay where he had abandoned them.

Hickok struck a long match with his thumbnail and touched the moist wick of the lamp on his desk before adjusting the flame until it was bright enough to light up the entire office. Before discarding the burning wooden taper he touched the end of his cigar which had remained in the corner of his mouth for hours.

He sucked in the smoke and blew out the match before starting to check the photographic images on the posters. Most were pitifully poor but his now agile mind seemed to remember one face he had seen the night before.

It took only a few minutes for the marshal to locate the poster again and this time give it the consideration it deserved earlier.

The photograph on the poster was of a seated figure in an expensive studio setting. Holding the picture to the lantern, Hickok began to smile.

'Wilson Penny known as Tulsa.' Wild Bill read the name off the poster before getting to the best part. 'Wanted Dead or Alive: $1,000.'

Hickok leaned back in his chair and held the piece of paper above his head as he began reading the details.

'Known to ride with a gang of bank and train-robbers headed by an outlaw answering only to the name of Black. Other gang members unknown. Tulsa has weakness for poker and is prone to cheat.' Bill Hickok raised his boots on to the desk and began to laugh as he thought about the reward money.

In Abilene $1,000 went an awful long way. He had begun to think of how many ways there were to spend such a sum when the clock on his wall chimed.

Looking up, he noted the time was a quarter past five. He swung his legs off the desk, planted his boots firmly on the floor and stood up. He folded the Wanted poster neatly, tucked it into his jacket-pocket, leaned over the lamp and blew into its glass funnel to extinguish its flame.

He locked the door behind him and headed through the shadows along the street towards his hotel.

TWELVE

Sunrise saw the streets of Abilene almost empty except for the figure of McQueen as he led three saddled horses towards the rear of the Taverstock Hotel. He had done what he had set out to do. He had completed the first stage of the plan which had brought him and his companions to Abilene, the plan which had been devised by their dead partner, Tulsa. As he moved through the shadows that the morning sun had yet to obliterate, he felt the alarm rising in his soul which had been suppressed until this very moment. He had done everything as instructed by Black, who seemed determined to follow the detailed plans left to them by Tulsa.

McQueen took a deep sigh before tying the three horses he had obtained securely to a wooden upright in the shade of an alley behind the hotel.

Checking the saddles before entering the back door of the Taverstock, McQueen moved quickly for a man who had not had any sleep, to the rear stairs, avoiding any prying eyes from the hotel's lobby. Taking the steps of the stairs two at a time, he reached the rooms where his partners waited. As the sweating McQueen opened the door he found Grainger and Black staring out of one of the open windows.

As usual, both men had totally different expressions etched across their faces. Grainger looked worried and Black seemed exhilarated.

'I got the three fastest mounts at the livery, boys,' McQueen announced as he walked into the room. He headed straight for the table and a nearly empty whiskey bottle. He poured himself a three-fingers measure.

'How can you be sure?' Grainger asked, rubbing his sore eyes as he turned to face the drinking man.

McQueen smiled, lowered his glass from his lips and pulled out a blood-covered razor-sharp stiletto from his pants pocket.

'Ain't a horse in the livery ever going to be able to do nothing again but limp, Grainger. I made sure of that.'

'Good.' Black nodded as he rose and joined McQueen at the table. He poured himself a drink. 'Just like old Tulsa planned it.'

'There are other horses in Abilene,' Grainger fretted. 'The streets are full of them, outside every whorehouse and saloon.'

'Not many good ones. None of them match the three I got for us,' McQueen snapped.

'A cut cinch-strap here and there can slow even the fastest horses, Grainger,' Black said as he savoured the flavour of his drink. 'If you paid attention to the plans, you might not be so damn scared all the time.'

'I ain't scared. I'm just double-checking,' Grainger protested through the sweat which flowed from his pores like rain.

'I spent an hour using this knife on every bridle and cinch on every horse tied up outside every damn building in this town, Grainger,' McQueen growled as he walked to the open window waving the bloody blade at the nervous man. 'I figure there ain't nobody going to follow us.'

'Perfect.' Black chuckled.

'I reckon we still need a fourth man to take Tulsa's place if this job is going to pan out, Black,' Grainger ventured. 'The plan is for a quartet, not a trio.'

McQueen looked across at Black. 'Grainger could be right.'

Black shook his head. 'There ain't no fourth man and it's too late for us to try and find one. Besides, Tulsa was the brains but he never done much on the actual practical side. The robbing has always been down to us three, ain't it?'

'He was a good man to have holding the horses. Tulsa never chickened out when the shooting started, did he?' Grainger rubbed the sweat off his face with a handkerchief. It seemed a pointless exercise.

'Tulsa had guts OK,' Black agreed.

'He was a good man to clear the streets.' McQueen recalled how Tulsa had had a way of scaring people off a street by shooting at everyone and anything during their numerous bank raids. It was a job which took nerve and a special sort of man to do properly.

'This ain't a bank job, boys. I figure we can manage without old Tulsa this time.' Black brooded as he began to wonder exactly how valuable their late partner might have been over the years they had ridden together.

'It does mean we have to trim his plan a tad, though.' The face of McQueen showed his own doubts as he spoke.

Black poured himself another drink. 'Just a tad.'

'And there's Hickok. Tulsa never made any provision for Wild Bill when he devised his plan.' Grainger stood and felt the pants of his expensive suit cling to his damp legs.

'As far as I can figure, Hickok don't even wake

up before noon on a good day. We will have the whole thing sewn up before he gets his pants on.' Black tried to convince himself as well as the others as he spoke over the rim of his whiskey glass. 'He was up half the night keeping cowboys on the straight and narrow. He might not even get out of bed before sundown.'

McQueen's chest heaved.

'I hope you're right, Black. I sure hope you're right.'

THIRTEEN

It was almost noon and the town of Abilene was still barely awake. Only storekeepers seemed to rise early in this strange dusty cattle town. Storekeepers and businessmen on a mission to buy vast numbers of prime Texan steers. The three outlaws stood opposite the grand edifice known as the Cattlemen's Club watching the men dressed in Eastern-style suits entering the impressive building.

After crossing the wide street Black led his two companions into the large brick building where the cattle agents had gathered in eager anticipation of getting the best prices for their Eastern bosses. None of the three seemed out of place in the presence of so many well-dressed men.

They wore the same style of clothing as the legitimate traders and it seemed as if they were almost invisible to the eyes of men who had other things on their minds. You could smell the tension in the air as so many agents began to get more and more excited as the hour approached.

A large clock on the marble wall attracted all the men's attention as the huge minute-hand drew ever closer to the top of the clock face.

Black studied the hall carefully as he leaned against its polished marble walls. It matched Tulsa's description exactly. McQueen moved through the anxious agents as he too checked that everything was where it was supposed to be.

It was.

Apart from the large ten-foot-high double-doors by which they had entered, the hall had three other smaller doors, one to the right-hand side and two on the back wall on either side of the raised platform.

It all tallied perfectly. Tulsa had had many faults but when it came to detail, he had been an artist.

Grainger stayed close to Black and tried to remain as cool as the room itself. It was an impossible task for the man who had always been the weak link in Black's gang. Self-doubt was something he had always been prone to during his years with Black but there was a very good reason why it was tolerated.

'The room matches Tulsa's plan,' Black noted as

he studied the scraps of paper in his hand.

Grainger nodded. He was always scared before a job but he had never been as utterly terrified as he was at this moment. As he watched the door to the left of the platform open he felt physically sick.

All three of the hardened robbers watched from the rear of the hall as a small bald man came from the open doorway between a pair of armed guards, who were big by anyone's standards. They carried a huge metal cash-box between them.

Black raised himself on to his toes and looked over the heads of the cattle agents, who seemed to be drawn towards the small figure as he mounted the raised platform, like moths to a naked flame.

Black turned to McQueen. 'Two guards just like Tulsa said.'

'They got scatter-guns.' McQueen frowned. 'Messy things if you get in their way.'

'That could work to our advantage,' Black whispered. 'It ain't the sort of weaponry to use when there are so many innocent folks around.'

McQueen began to smile. 'Reckon so. If them meatheads let loose with a scatter-gun they'd probably kill or wound half the cattle agents as well as us.'

Grainger reached under his jacket and checked his pistol in the shoulder holster.

'I could take out both them guards before they

had time to blink, Black,' he muttered confidently.

'That's why I tolerate you, Grainger. You are the best shot it has been my good fortune to encounter.' Black patted the man on his shoulder. 'I think this job will be easier than I originally anticipated.'

'How come?' McQueen asked as the bald man started the bidding for the massive herd.

'Those guards have been chosen for their muscle and not their gun skills,' Black replied. He listened with great interest as the bidding for the first stock-pen of steers was resolved.

'When do we strike, Black?' Grainger asked eagerly.

'When the last bid has been made and the cash has been placed in the strongbox, Grainger,' Black answered coldly. He turned to McQueen who was lighting a cigar. 'Now go and get our horses and bring them to the rear of this building, just as we rehearsed.'

'Be there in no more than five minutes,' Grainger added, beginning to toy with the pistol beneath his left arm – a weapon he was expert with.

'I'll be there, boys,' McQueen said, touching the brim of his hat.

McQueen blew the ash from his cigar and strolled out of the huge cool building into the brilliant sunshine. As he headed slowly across the wide street to where he had left their three horses McQueen's attention was drawn to the two dusty riders who were heading into Abilene from the south.

Although he had never set eyes upon either rider before, he felt as if their unexpected arrival could mean only one thing.

Trouble.

He reached the opposite side of the wide street and stepped up on to the boardwalk outside the Taverstock Hotel, where he paused and watched Tom Dix and Dan Shaw ride silently down the hot street in the direction of the marshal's office.

McQueen's keen eyes focused on the holster and the exposed sleek pistol-grip that hugged Tom Dix's thigh over his leather chaps as he rode casually by.

For a moment McQueen's mind raced. Were these outlaws intent on doing what he, Black and Grainger were about to do? Were these two riders part of a bigger gang intent on grabbing the auction money?

A thousand questions flashed through the young man's mind as his eyes trailed the two riders.

Were they the law? Had Hickok got himself a couple of deputies that they knew nothing about?

Whoever the two riders might be, they were yet another threat to Tulsa's well-thought-out plan.

Like the unexpected presence of Wild Bill Hickok, they could tip the odds against McQueen and his partners.

For a brief moment McQueen considered running back to the Cattlemen's Club and telling Black of the two strangers' arrival. Then he realized there was no time.

He had to get the horses and be at the rear of the huge brick building in a matter of only minutes. Sweat began to run freely down his face.

Throwing his cigar away, McQueen turned and ran along the boardwalk until he reached the corner of the hotel. He jumped down into the dust and headed speedily up the side of the large building. A few minutes earlier his mind had been focused on only one thing; now, as his legs carried him swiftly to the waiting horses, he was worried.

There were only two riders, but they looked as if they knew how to handle themselves.

As his sweating hands untied the three sets of reins McQueen felt his heart pounding within his chest. The two strangers who had just ridden into Abilene had horses and saddles he had not tampered with.

What would Black do when he was told? There was no time to sabotage them now.

Dragging the three skittish horses behind him towards the sun-baked street, McQueen began to fear that everything was now balanced on a knife-edge.

FOURTEEN

It was a strangely confident Grainger who followed Black unnoticed through the door to the right of the platform in the massive hall of the Cattlemen's Club. Black quickly closed the door behind them and drew his gun. He looked around the dark corridor which led to the strongroom. Grainger pulled his own pistol from its hiding-place beneath his left arm and nodded to the grim-featured Black.

Black recognized the layout of the narrow corridor from Tulsa's precise description. He waved his gun for Grainger to follow.

The two men moved stealthily down to where they knew the strongroom was located. The door was wide open, the way it had been left by the auctioneer and his pair of guards a few minutes earlier.

Like the deadly but skilled thieves they were, Grainger and Black entered the room and soon managed to press themselves into the darkest of its corners.

They knew there were only a few lots remaining for the cattle agents to bid for and time was now ticking relentlessly down to the end of the auction.

Black pointed with his pistol at the rear door. This door, according to their plans, led out into the dusty sun-baked expanse opposite the railtracks and the vast stock-pens filled with the cattle brought to Kansas all the way from the fertile Texas pastures.

Then a noise echoed around the small room. For a moment the two outlaws glanced at one another as they both realized it was the sound of the agents within the hall. Then the sound ceased and was replaced by the footsteps of approaching men.

The bald auctioneer entered the room first and headed straight for the open safe, whilst the two burly guards struggled with the heavy strongbox behind him.

Swiftly, the deadly Grainger closed and locked the office door as the two lumbering men reached the safe with their heavy burden.

Startled, all three men gazed behind them into the barrels of the .45s trained upon them.

Black indicated with the barrel of his pistol for

the two guards to lower the strongbox on to the floor and drop their scatter-guns.

They complied.

Then, faster than the blink of an eye, Grainger fanned his gun-hammer and placed a bullet into each of the huge guards' skulls.

Blood spattered across the room as the men fell to the ground. Most of it covered the terrified bald man who cowered beside the safe as he watched the outlaws approaching him.

'Unlock the box. Now.' Black shouted his order at the trembling figure as Grainger released the bolts of the rear door and checked that McQueen was where he should be.

McQueen was waiting atop one of the trio of horses with the heavy saddle-bags over his free arm.

'He's there,' Grainger informed his partner in a voice which reflected his fervour at killing again.

Black watched as the bald auctioneer unlocked the heavy padlock and then opened the lid of the strongbox, revealing a fortune in crisp large-denomination bills.

'Get the bags, Grainger,' Black ordered his associate.

Grainger ran out and grabbed the three saddle-bags from the mounted McQueen before returning into the small office.

'Fill them, fast,' Black said as he stared at the

door which led out to the rest of the huge Cattleman's Club. A door which was beginning to rock as frenzied fists began trying to smash it down. 'Hurry.'

Grainger holstered his pistol and used both his hands to drag the cash into one bag as the stunned auctioneer filled another.

Black aimed his Colt at the centre of the door and fired a bullet straight through it. The banging stopped for a few seconds before resuming with increased intensity.

Grainger buckled the leather straps on one set of saddle-bags, then he began to help the bald man fill the third one.

'I told you we needed a fourth man to replace Tulsa.'

Black cocked his gun at the door again and sent another bullet through its solid heart. This time the muffled sound of a scream greeted his ears.

'Done?' Black asked. He backed away from the door before firing again.

Grainger secured the last of the bag-flaps and picked all three up off the floor.

'Come on, Black,' Grainger said. He exited the rear doorway and began tying the bags to the saddle cantles of the three mounts held in check by McQueen.

Black sent two more shots into the door before stepping over one of the blood-soaked bodies and staring down at the kneeling bald figure. Without even blinking he cocked his gun hammer and squeezed the trigger. The man crashed forward as his life ended abruptly on the floor.

Black rushed out of the open doorway, expelled his spent shells, and accepted the reins from McQueen. As his right leg went over the saddle Black straightened up and crammed bullets into his Colt .45.

All three riders turned their horses and rode over the gleaming railtracks away into the distance.

'You ain't an easy man to find, Wild Bill,' Dan Shaw said. He drew the reins of his black gelding up to his chest and stopped the big horse beside the hitching rail outside the hotel. The tall figure of James Butler Hickok stepped out into the baking sunshine.

'Sometimes it pays for folks not to know where you are,' Hickok said, staring hard at the rider.

'We went to the marshal's office first.' Shaw rubbed the grime from his face.

'Do I know you, stranger?' Hickok asked as he placed a long thin cigar between his teeth and stared at Tom Dix riding towards them.

'Think back about twelve years,' Shaw said as Dix stopped his mount beside him.

'Hell, I can't remember what happened twelve

days ago.' Wild Bill Hickok smiled as his attention was drawn across to the men who were rushing from the massive Cattlemen's Club building and heading in their direction.

'You remember me, Bill?' Tom Dix asked. He removed his Stetson and hung it on his saddle horn.

Hickok looked straight at the face of the man on the brown gelding and suddenly began to dismiss all the grey hair and wrinkles which now covered it.

'Dix?'

'For a minute there I thought you'd forgotten me, Bill,' Dix said. He studied the impressive figure who did not appear to have aged a day since their last encounter.

'How could I forget the one man who saved my life, Dix?'

Tom Dix nodded and pointed at Shaw. 'Remember Dan?'

'Dan Shaw,' Hickok nodded.

'Marshal!' The name was called out frantically several times by the figures who ran towards Hickok as he moved away from Dix and Dan.

Hickok's head lowered as he stared down from the boardwalk at the group of men who approached.

'Marshal Hickok, quick!' a voice yelled from amid the group of frenzied men.

'You boys look like you seen a ghost.'

'Somebody just robbed the Cattlemen's Club,' the familiar voice of the store-owner Don McKay announced.

Hickok ran his thumbnail over the tip of his match and pulled the exploding flame to his cigar. He puffed thoughtfully for several seconds as he concentrated on the gathering before him. Several men were covered in blood and wood-splinters.

'Anyone killed?' Dix leaned across in his saddle and looked down at the men.

'A few folks got wounded when the robbers shot through the office door,' a large man said.

'We haven't been able to get into the strong-room to find out what happened to Mr Soloman,' McKay added.

'Who is he?' Hickok asked through the trail of smoke which drifted from his mouth.

'That's the auctioneer, Wild Bill,' another voice said.

'You mean the little bald guy?' Hickok sucked on his cigar as he watched Dix and Shaw moving their horses closer to the hotel's boardwalk.

'You need some help, Bill?' Dix asked.

Hickok smiled and patted the shoulder of the man who had once saved his life. 'I never turn down the help of a friend, Dix.'

Dix cast a glance at Dan Shaw. Shaw was nodding with a smile on his face.

'Good job I never went to sleep last night.' Hickok watched as the two dust-caked riders dismounted. 'Otherwise I might be tired.'

'Is there another way into the office?' Shaw heard himself ask as his years as a peace keeper surfaced.

'Sure is,' McKay replied. 'There's a door around back next to the railtracks.'

Hickok stepped purposefully down from the boardwalk and moved through the men as he headed toward the large brick building which was now being besieged by curious citizens.

'Come on, boys. Let's take us a look.'

FIFTEEN

It was a gruesome sight by anyone's standards within the small office. Wild Bill Hickok stood flanked by his trusted Dix and Shaw in the frame of the rear door to the strong-room of the Cattlemen's Club. The scene of brutal carnage was already attracting flies as the tall figure moved reluctantly towards the bodies. Blood covered a quarter of the floor area as Hickok leaned over the three bodies and inspected the fatal wounds in more detail.

He had never been one to inspect such things in the past but with the crowd behind him, Wild Bill felt as if he ought to try and get some idea of what sort of killers they were looking for.

It was obvious this was no simple murder and robbery but a carefully planned execution. These three men had not stood a chance. From the time the outlaws had entered this room, it was clear they intended leaving no witnesses.

Hickok's hooded eyes stared down into the empty strongbox before he turned and walked back out into the sun.

'Last time I seen a bloody mess like that was back in Hays City,' Hickok said. 'I caused that one. this is much neater. Whoever shot these guards was one hell of a shot. One bullet in each of the heads ain't easy.'

Dix shook his head.

'How much money was taken?'

'Who can tell?' Hickok shrugged as he faced the crowd beside them. 'Anyone have any idea how much money was raised at the auction?'

One of the cattle agents stepped forward. 'I figure close to twenty thousand dollars, Marshal.'

Hickok glanced at Shaw and then Dix. 'That's a big piece of change, boys.'

'Paper money?' Dan Shaw asked the agent.

'Yes sir,' came the reply.

'Damn,' Hickok snapped as he put the cigar between his lips and inhaled deeply. 'If it had been gold coin it would have slowed the varmints up a tad.'

Dix rubbed his chin. 'Who could have done this, Bill?'

Hickok pulled out the folded Wanted poster from his jacket pocket and handed it to the shorter man.

'Tulsa? Did he do this?' Dix asked.

'Not him. His gang.' Hickok sucked on the long cigar as he rested his spine against the wall of the building and stared at the blue sky above them.

'How can you be sure this Tulsa didn't do this?' Shaw asked, looking over Dix's shoulder at the Wanted poster.

'I already killed Tulsa,' Hickok said through the smoke that trailed from his mouth. 'That must have been why he was in Abilene, to plan this job for the rest of his gang.'

Dix gave the poster back to the marshal and studied the ground around them.

'I ain't sure, but it looks like there were three riders.'

Shaw agreed. 'I'd say you're right, Dixie. Looks like three horses were waiting outside here.'

Hickok moved away from the wall and ran his fingers through his hair. 'Guess we better get our horses and start trailing these bastards.'

Just then a young lad came running up to the crowd. He pushed his way through until he found the marshal.

'Pop told me to come and tell you that somebody maimed all the horses in the livery, Wild Bill.'

Hickok's eyes narrowed as he stared down at the child.

'Did they get my horse, son?'

'Yes, sir.' The boy shuffled his bare feet. 'He's

lame just like the rest in Pop's livery.'

'Somebody took a razor to most of the saddles in town,' an angry cowboy announced as he strode up to the marshal. 'Who's going to pay for the repairs?'

'This gang sure had things organized, Bill,' Dan Shaw said as he stared out at the arid plain beyond the railtracks.

Hickok looked at the men behind the stable lad. 'Find me a horse, boys. The fastest horse there is. I got to catch me some vermin.'

'You want company?' Dix asked Hickok.

'The three of us could sure make them *hombres* a tad scared, Wild Bill.' Shaw rested a hand on Tom Dix's shoulder as he watched the face of the stone-faced marshal.

'If they know Wild Bill Hickok's on their trail, I figure they're already nervous, Dan,' Dix said as he watched the looming figure in the frock-coat move between them.

'Let's try and find me a horse, boys.' James Butler Hickok tossed away his cigar and walked between the two men back towards Main Street. 'A tall horse with some vinegar in it.'

SIXTEEN

The three riders thundered across the almost flat ground side by side. Dust rose from the flashing hoofs into the still air and hung there as if unable to obey the laws of gravity. None of the riders had dared look back since they had headed out of Abilene with blood on their hands and a fortune in their saddle-bags. A dozen or more miles of hard dust-covered ground would have deterred most sane men, but not the trio of outlaws. They had to seek a place marked on the plans by their late comrade Tulsa.

Black led his two companions across the vast baking plain in the direction marked on his precious map. The horses were well chosen and well up to the task in hand as their hoofs ate up the dry unforgiving terrain.

It seemed as if they had been riding for a thousand lifetimes as they began to climb a ridge. At last the three horses began to slow as they completed their climb.

The three riders dragged their mounts to a halt on the crest of the ridge, dismounted and stared back at the trail of dust behind them.

It was their own dust.

There was no sign of anyone else back there.

'They ain't following, Black.' Grainger laughed as he pulled his canteen off the saddle and unscrewed its stopper.

'How could they? McQueen fixed it just as Tulsa wrote on our plan.' Black felt exhilarated as he spoke.

McQueen squared up to Black. 'Two riders came into town just as I was getting our horses from behind the hotel.'

'Two riders came into Abilene as you were getting our horses, you say?' Black repeated the sentence which left a sour taste in his mouth.

'Yep. Two sun-baked riders came riding in. I had no time to fix their horses because I had to get to the back of the Cattlemen's Club.' McQueen felt a shiver trace his spine as he listened to his own words drip from his dry lips.

Grainger swallowed a mouthful of water before moving towards the two men standing toe to toe.

'Who were they?'

McQueen glanced at Grainger. 'I don't know.

They could have been outlaws like us or they might even have been deputies.'

Black rubbed his face. 'No call to panic over two varmints.'

Grainger agreed. 'They were probably just a couple of drifters.'

'The one closest to me wore a fancy shooting-rig. He wasn't no cowpuncher,' McQueen recalled as he removed his own canteen from the saddle horn and opened its stopper. 'I seen guns like that before.'

'Gunfighters?' Black mused.

'That would be my bet, Black.' McQueen nodded as he raised the canteen to his lips and drank freely from it.

'If they were gunfighters, Hickok might just tangle with them instead of us, boys,' Black suggested.

Grainger stared back at the trail they had left through the sun-hardened ground. There was still no sign of anyone following them.

'Ain't nobody coming, boys.'

Black bit his lip. 'How could they?'

'Hickok might get one of the horses off the two men who came into town, Black,' McQueen suggested.

'I figure if that had been the case, we'd see dust trailing us by now. There ain't nobody on our trail.' Black pointed at the empty plain behind them before turning to face the equally bleak landscape that lay ahead. 'No matter. All we have to do is continue on for another hour or so and all our troubles will be over.'

'Are you sure there's a town out there?' Grainger asked the older man as he hung his canteen back on the saddle horn.

Black help up the scraps of paper which had guided them so fruitfully.

'I ain't, but Tulsa was. He says in these plans that there's a place out there called Spring City. Plenty of water and plenty of fresh horses to buy.'

All three men mounted their lathered-up horses.

'Tulsa was a genius in his way,' Grainger admitted.

'That's exactly what he was. A genius,' Black agreed. He tapped his spurs into the sides of his mount and began leading his men onward into the dry plain before them.

Hickok soon found out that Black, McQueen and Grainger had done a pretty good job of sabotaging each and every one of the saddles in Abilene. This, combined with the mutilation of his fine horse as well as all the others within the huge livery stable, had given the outlaws exactly what they wanted: time to get away. With all the decent horseflesh maimed and only cowboys' quarter horses left, things appeared bleak to everyone.

Everyone except Wild Bill Hickok himself. He alone seemed less concerned than anyone that Black's gang were getting further and further away with every passing heartbeat.

It took nearly an hour to find anything resembling a reliable horse capable of a long hard ride. Cowboy horses tended to be bred to walk, a feat they did well. But it seemed a doubtful bet that any of them could actually reach a gallop let alone maintain one.

During the time Hickok's friends had tried to find him a fast mount, Pop Larson, the livery stable owner, had worked feverishly to repair one of the damaged saddles.

For the sixty odd minutes during which all this had been occurring, Hickok had stood propping up the bar within the Drover's Rest Saloon staring at a bottle of whiskey whilst Tom Dix and Dan Shaw consumed two steak dinners.

'You going to have a drink, Bill?' Dix asked, wiping his mouth with the chequered napkin. He swivelled around in his hard-back chair.

Hickok turned around and looked down at his two smiling companions. Men he had not set eyes upon in over a decade and yet men he trusted beyond any others.

'Reckon I should take a drink or two but I just ain't in the mood,' Hickok replied as he strolled over to the table where his friends were seated.

'How come?' Dan asked, mopping up the gravy on his plate with a chunk of bread.

'Whiskey tends to put me in a good mood lately,' Hickok began. Then, through the large window, he saw a saddled horse being led toward the saloon by Pop Larson. 'This ain't a job for somebody who happens to be in a good mood. This is a job for a man with a mean temper.'

Suddenly all three men's attention was drawn to the window. They too saw the figure of Pop Larson leading the saddled cowboy horse towards them.

'There's your replacement horse, Bill.' Dix pointed as he stood and plucked his hat off the back of his chair.

'Ain't much of a horse for a man with long legs, boys,' Wild Bill observed as he headed for the swing doors.

The three men stood on the saloon boardwalk as the old livery owner tied the animal up to the hitching rail beside the two geldings of Dix and Shaw.

'The saddle cinch will hold. I fixed the bridle too,' Larson said, wheezing like a man who had inhaled a lot of trail dust in his day.

Hickok tossed him a silver dollar.

'That's mighty fine, Pop. Mighty fine.'

All three watched as the livery man walked

away in the direction of his stables once more.

'It is a tad short in the leg, Bill,' Shaw said. He stepped down and inspected the horse which had been borrowed from one of the young cowboys Hickok had reprimanded during the previous night.

Hickok shook his head as he too stepped down and walked around the animal.

'My boots will drag along the ground when I get in the saddle, boys,' he moaned.

Dix grinned as he watched Don McKay coming towards them carrying six full canteens of fresh water, exactly as he had been instructed.

'I got them, Wild Bill. Just like you told me,' McKay gasped as he handed the canteens over to the men.

'Thank you kindly, Don,' said Hickok. He proceeded to hang two canteens on each of the saddle horns.

'Two canteens each, Bill?' Dix queried as he stepped down and stooped under the hitching rail. 'How come?'

Hickok turned and stared down in the direction of the rail-head and pointed to the arid land that lay beyond.

'Them outlaws were mighty slick. They staged the perfect robbery. Killed all the witnesses and made a clean getaway, but they did one thing wrong.'

'What did they do wrong, Bill?' asked Dix. He watched the face of the tall marshal start to smile.

'They headed out to a town called Spring City.' Hickok shook his head.

'So?' Dan Shaw rested his hands on the grips of his guns as he listened.

'Spring City is a ghost town since a real bad storm two months ago. The wells collapsed and everybody just up and left. There ain't another town or water-hole for about fifty miles in that direction, boys.'

Dix began to nod. 'So they think they can get themselves fresh water and probably fresh horses there?'

'They could have got both up until the storm wiped out Spring City, Dix.' Hickok opened his pocket watch and studied the time. It was twenty minutes after one.

'That'll be a real painful surprise for them varmints.' Dix scratched at his whiskered chin.

'That's why I ain't been too worried about chasing them. We got all the time in the world.' Hickok snapped the watch-cover shut and slid it into his vest pocket.

'We might even bump into them coming back.'

'I sure hope so.' Hickok was about to step into the stirrup of the small cowboy horse when Dan handed the reins of his tall black gelding to the marshal.

'Figure even your legs ain't going to drag along the ground if you ride my horse, Bill,' Shaw said.

'Are you sure, Dan?' Dix smiled as he stepped into his stirrup and hauled himself atop the brown horse. 'Bill has got pretty long legs.'

'Thanks, Dan.' Hickok patted Dan's shoulder as he mounted the black gelding.

'My pleasure, Bill.' As the words fell from Dan Shaw's cracked lips he saw the giant figure gather the reins in his hands, then suddenly turn in his direction. There was a sparkle in the hooded eyes.

'Has he got vinegar?'

'Plenty of vinegar, Bill.' Dan smiled as he mounted the cowboy horse and turned it around to face the railtracks.

'Let's ride, boys.' Hickok pulled his reins to the left and spurred the black horse into a canter. Dix and Shaw rode to either side of the legendary marshal as they headed out of Abilene and on towards Spring City.

SEVENTEEN

Black and his ruthless cohorts drove their exhausted horses on and on at breakneck speed as they caught sight of the bleached wooden buildings through the heat haze. They had shown their mounts no mercy in their bid to reach this haven where they expected to find not only fresh horses but an abundance of crystal-clear water.

'Spring City, boys!' yelled Black excitedly at the top of his lungs. He dug his spurs deep into the flesh of his sweat-lathered steed.

All three riders began to drive their weary horses far beyond the poor creatures' capabilities into the silent street between the array of deserted structures. For a few moments, as the dust which greeted their arrival swirled around them, they did not notice anything untoward. Then as they sat in their saddles outside the large saloon and the air began to clear, the reality of the situation dawned on them. McQueen said nothing as he swivelled around in his high saddle, observing the dreadful silence around them.

Black dismounted and wrapped his reins around the hitching rail before staring into the empty water-trough. His expression altered from one of glee to one of total confusion. Grabbing the handle of the pump. Black began to use every ounce of his strength, vainly trying to get water to pour from its cast-iron opening. There was nothing.

'What's going on here, Black?' asked Grainger as he slid from his saddle and moved next to the sweating man. 'Is this the right town?'

'This is Spring City all right,' muttered Black. He rubbed his hands together, trying to rid them of the red rust-stains from the pump handle.

McQueen looked around at all the deserted buildings again. His face seemed emotionless. There was no sign of life in this place.

'This town is deserted,' McQueen told his companions bluntly without seeming to care one way or another.

'It has been for quite some time by the looks of it,' the troubled Grainger chipped in.

'No! It ain't possible. It just ain't. There has to be a mistake, boys.' Black quickly mounted the boardwalk and defiantly entered the saloon through its swing doors. He was followed by both his confederates.

'Reckon you're right about there being a mistake, Black,' McQueen sighed. 'And we made it.'

All three stood inside the empty saloon staring around the dust-filled building. The long bar remained, as did all the tables and chairs. Yet there was not one living creature to be seen or heard.

Black dragged a chair out from beneath a table and planted himself on it.

'How can this be?'

McQueen walked around the saloon before accepting the fact there was no alcohol left. It had gone with the residents of Spring City.

'I thought Tulsa said this was a town full of folks?'

'That's what Tulsa said in the plan, boys,' said Black, shaking his head in disbelief. 'I don't get it.'

'I do.' McQueen hovered over Black. 'Tulsa made a mistake.'

Black looked up. 'A pretty big one.'

'Big enough,' McQueen nodded.

Grainger rubbed his neck as his eyes focused on their horses standing in the last of the day's sunshine.

'We rode them nags into the ground getting here so we could buy fresh ones. I ain't sure we are going to find any fresh mounts here.'

'I'm more scared we ain't going to find us any water,' McQueen interrupted.

Black rose to his feet, swung on his heels and marched out into the barren street. His eyes tracked along all of the buildings in his line of sight. None seemed to show any hint of occupancy.

'First, we check every damn water pump in this town. If there's one drop of water, find it.'

Grainger shook his head. 'I got me a feeling that something real bad happened here.'

'Bad enough to make an entire community cut and run,' Black said coldly as the sound of thunder rumbled across the sky above them.

'Thunder.' McQueen stared up at the darkening heavens. 'If we are lucky, it might just rain.'

Black rubbed his lips. 'I sure in hell hope so, boys.'

McQueen struck a match and lit his short fat cigar. Then he pointed up at the darkening sky.

'Come on. The way our luck's running, it won't rain.'

'We better try and find some water.' Grainger frowned as he stepped down into the street.

All three men headed in different directions, seeking water. It would not take long before they would realize the futility of their quest.

James Butler Hickok continued riding ahead of

his two pals as darkness overwhelmed them. Even as lightning forked across the black sky above, and thunder seemed to explode all around them, they pushed on towards Spring City. Hickok knew he had two of the best men with him and was also aware that three of the most evil men waited out there on the plains. His was not the spirit of a man who ever allowed anything to slow his methodical progress.

As the storm raged above the heads of the trio of riders, they slowed their pace to little better than a canter. They knew their horses needed water if they were to keep going in this merciless place.

Tom Dix drew his brown gelding alongside the tall marshal and glanced at the face illuminated by the half-moon above them. It was a face which never seemed to alter.

'You figure we'll get there before sunrise, Wild Bill?' Dix asked as he stroked the neck of his calm trusty horse.

Hickok glanced down as another white flash of electricity splintered across the heavens. Both outriders glanced nervously up, but not Wild Bill Hickok, he sat staring ahead.

'Sure.'

Dan Shaw managed to get the small cowboy horse to draw level with his friends as the sound of an angry sky almost burst their eardrums.

'How far is it now?'

'There's still quite a way to go, Dan,' replied Hickok. He sat like a statue in the saddle and allowed the black gelding to make slow progress beneath him. There was no hurry, he thought. No hurry at all.

Hickok knew the three deadly men ahead of them had nowhere to go and all the time in the world to go there. They must have found out the bitter secret of Spring City by now, he concluded as he stared out into the blackness before them. They had to be getting thirsty by now and their horses must be exhausted. There was nothing those cold-blooded killers could do but sit and wait for dawn. Then they had to make a decision. They either had to return to Abilene or die slowly of thirst out there in the middle of nowhere.

As long as it did not rain.

Hickok prayed it would not rain and allow his foes to refresh themselves for the conflict ahead. They had to be on their knees with swollen tongues filling their mouths. Nothing less would suit the stone-faced marshal.

They deserved nothing better.

Bill Hickok knew the outlaws would not have to make their choice because he intended reaching the parched ghost town before sunrise and confronting them.

Dead or alive, the neatly folded Wanted poster for their partner Tulsa had said. As far as Hickok was concerned, what was good enough for their dead colleague was good enough for them.

'This reminds me of the time when we chased them riverboat robbers, Bill,' Dix shouted out.

'That was a long time ago, Dix.' Wild Bill recalled the night when the quiet rider had shown his grit and saved his life with an unmatched display of gunplay. 'I remember getting shot that night.'

'Sure was a long while ago,' Dix agreed. 'Ever been winged since?'

'Nope.'

'We were all a lot young then,' Dan called out from his bouncing cowboy horse as it grew weary beneath him.

'I hope you ain't implying I'm getting old, Dan?' The marshal stared down at the struggling mount and its rider.

'Well, me and Dixie are sure a tad older,' Dan laughed.

'You boys are, but I ain't.' Wild Bill Hickok began to slow his mount.

'Wild Bill is a legend, Dan. They don't age like us mortal critters.' Tom Dix began to pull his gelding up.

'Have you still got vinegar, Dix?' Hickok asked with a wry smile across his impressive features as he stopped the big black horse. The eerie dark sky began flashing and crackling above them again as the storm grew in intensity.

'He's still got plenty of vinegar, Bill,' Dan answered for his quieter friend. 'And he ain't lost any of his skill with them guns either.'

'He'll need every ounce of those skills before this is over, Dan.' The words from Wild Bill Hickok's mouth seemed to chill the air as they all dismounted.

'Time to water the horses, I guess,' said Dan. He dropped his hat onto the ground and took a canteen from his saddle, while holding the reins of the nervous cowboy horse in check.

Hickok held onto his reins as he stood staring out into the darkness ahead of them. He no longer trusted his eyes because they had lied to him many times since the war.

'Shall I water your mount, Bill?' Tom Dix asked the thoughtful figure.

Hickok removed his ten-gallon hat and handed it over without saying a word. For a brief moment he thought he had seen an unearthly glowing light out there on the silent black horizon. As he strained his eyes they refused to focus and he felt the terror returning to his soul.

Not now. The vision could not fail him now, he thought.

'What's wrong, Bill?' Tom Dix asked as he

noticed the bead of sweat rolling down from Hickok's hairline and across his fine features.

'Can you see it, Dix?' Hickok pointed a thin finger in the direction of where he imagined he had seen the briefest glimpse of a light.

Tom Dix rubbed the dust from his own tired eyes.

'Yeah, I see it.'

'Good, I was worried my eyes were playing tricks on me again.' Hickok sighed heavily as he turned and stared into the honest face of Tom Dix. A face he could see properly.

Tom Dix turned and looked into the troubled face of the tall man beside him. He had heard that tone in his voice before. It was the sound of doubt.

'What's wrong with your eyes, Bill?'

Hickok rested a hand on the thin shoulder. 'They can get a tad ornery now and then. They're OK now.'

'See what, Dixie?' Dan asked as the plains shook around them under the shock waves of yet another chilling thunderclap.

'A light in a window about ten miles away,' Dix replied as he poured water from his canteen into the upturned hat for the horse to drink from.

Dan Shaw gazed out at the distance. 'I must be getting old because I can't see nothing out there.'

'Me and Bill can, Dan.'

'That's Spring City, boys,' Hickok said quietly, and he sighed with relief that his vision had returned.

EIGHTEEN

The storm had continued growing angrily above them as Hickok, Dix and Shaw reached the outskirts of Spring City. The ferocity of the deadly lightning forks as they traced across the night sky and twisted into the ground seemed undimmed by each passing moment. The storm had only one redeeming quality, it had not allowed a single drop of rain to fall onto the three thirsty outlaws ahead.

The tall marshal stepped off his high saddle and held onto his reins firmly as the black gelding tried desperately to flee the terrifying sights and sounds all around them.

Tom Dix dismounted his brown horse and gripped its bridle firmly as he stopped beside Hickok. Dan Shaw slid from his saddle and dragged his animal up to his companions.

Shoulder to shoulder they faced what lay in Spring City with little or no thought for their own safety.

The three had ridden wide on their approach to Spring City, so as not to catch the eye of any possible outlaw on sentry duty. As they walked their mounts over the last hundred yards of baked, hard ground, they all drew one of their pistols from their holsters in readiness.

As they reached the first of the town's deserted houses, James Butler Hickok paused and glanced down into the silent street. Tumbleweed rolled past them, driven by the storm which encircled this place.

Both Dix and Dan looked at the illuminated second-floor window of the saloon, where Hickok pointed his pistol barrel. It was half-way down the long dark street.

The marshal wrapped his reins around a wooden porch upright and secured them firmly. The storm had spooked their mounts into a lathered frenzy.

'They might be where the light is, but I sure doubt it,' Hickok said as his partners tied their own mounts to the same pole with equal firmness.

'There ain't no sight of their horses, Bill,' said Dan, as he stared down into the street.

'They probably bedded them down in the livery.' Hickok pointed his gun barrel at the wooden edifice beyond the last of the street's buildings.

Tom Dix rubbed his face and vainly tried to see if any of the gang were lying in wait for them.

'Smells like a trap to me, Bill.'

'Yep, they knew it was a fair chance someone might trail them from Abilene,' Dan said as he watched both his friends surveying the situation carefully from the corner of the wooden house.

'They could be holed up in any of these damn buildings,' Wild Bill said angrily.

'But which one?' Dix questioned.

'Let's try and find out.' The marshal was about to start walking when the sky above them lit up again and sheets of white lightning turned the night sky almost as bright as day.

Dix gripped his friend's shoulder and pulled him back a few steps.

'Look,' Dix said pointing out at the store-front opposite the saloon. Nature bathed it in its eerie light long enough for them to spot one of their enemies.

A figure was standing in a doorframe sucking on a cigar. It was McQueen.

'There's one of the dirty varmints, Bill,' Dan Shaw whispered.

'It is a trap,' Dix growled.

Hickok said nothing as he turned and led his two friends around the rear of the building into the blackest of shadows.

'Where we headed?' Dan asked and followed the two others through the darkness.

'Hush up and follow,' Hickok answered as he moved silently through the black gloom with the two men on his heels.

The marshal led his pals past the backs of five buildings until they came to a narrow alley between the saloon and another wooden structure. The storm grew angrier all around the trio as they paused at the very edge of the wall.

Leaning on the corner of the building, Wild Bill peered down the alley until his eyes adjusted and focused. McQueen was directly in line with the end of it.

'Do you reckon he's the only one awake, Bill?' Dix asked as he too stared at the figure hiding in the doorway of a store, apparently enjoying a smoke.

'Could be,' Hickok replied as he thought. 'It could also be that they are all hidden around town waiting for the posse to arrive.'

'Dry-gulching a posse would be a good way of getting their hands on water, I guess,' said Dix. 'What are we going to do?'

'I could plug that varmint from here but that would be real dumb,' Hickok drawled.

'There ain't no way to get behind that critter,' Tom Dix remarked. 'I figure we better try and locate the other two before deciding what to do.'

'They could be anywhere.' Dan shook his head.

'Yep. But if we draw that varmint's fire it'll give his partners time to get the drop on us,' Hickok said coldly.

'I figure we ought to keep moving to the other end of town and slowly edge our way back,' Dix suggested. 'We might flush them out of their hiding-places.'

Wild Bill nodded. 'Sounds good to me.'

Without saying another word the three men used the shadows to head around the rest of the buildings until they were at the very end of the long street. The sounds of the outlaws' horses could be heard inside the livery stable a few dozen yards away.

'Their horses are in the livery,' Dan nodded to his friends.

'I bet the money ain't, though,' Dix grinned.

Hickok drew both his pistols and allowed them to hang at arm's length whilst Dix and Shaw moved beside him.

'Fan out, boys,' Hickok instructed. 'You go to that side of the street, Dix. Dan, you keep to this side of the street. I want you boys to move down the boardwalks slowly.'

'What you going to do, Bill?' Dan asked.

'You'll see.' Hickok pulled his gun-hammers back with his thumbs until they locked. 'Now!'

Without one moment's hesitation, Tom Dix

crossed the street quickly with both his primed Colts in his hands as Dan remained close to the wall of the nearest building.

To both men's surprise, Wild Bill Hickok walked slowly to the centre of the wide street. He stood staring down its length as the sky lit up again above Spring City with nature's majestic fury.

It was an awesome sight.

Hickok looked like something from the bowels of hell itself as the brilliant lightning flashed over the town. Before the sound of the trailing thunder rumbled into earshot, the voices of the three startled outlaws could be heard echoing about the long street.

'It's Hickok!' exclaimed Black from within the darkened saloon as he recognized the legendary long mane of hair flapping in the swirling wind.

'How did he get here?' Grainger's pitiful question rang out from another doorway close to the saloon.

'Is he alone?' McQueen asked as he sucked calmly on his cigar.

Then before another word could be uttered by the gang of outlaws, the whole town shook as a deafening thunderclap exploded above them. It was like a million cannon shots from the Devil's own artillery to the ears of the six men dotted around Spring City.

Within seconds of the questions and before the ringing ear-splitting noise of the storm above them had ceased, the bullets from their guns began to explode down the street. Red flashes traced through the air from the outlaws' pistols as they tried to shoot the ghostlike image of Hickok.

Hickok moved as he always moved, deliberately. Not a step to his left nor to his right, but straight down the street towards the three gunmen.

It was almost suicidal in its simplicity but few if any other men would have had the courage to do what he had decided to do: walk straight down the middle of the street without any cover.

Dix ran along the dark boardwalk on one side of the street as Dan Shaw remained level with him on the other. Both returned the gang's fire.

'Take cover, Bill.' Dix's voice rang out at the marshal as he levelled his own shots in the direction of the outlaws.

Hickok seemed either oblivious to the danger or in total contempt of it. He neither ducked nor made any effort to shy away from the deadly lead which was being trained upon him as he continued walking down the street. It was as if he had an invisible shield protecting him as every bullet missed his tall lean frame.

It was only when Hickok was within a hundred yards of the guns that were shooting at him, one from the left side of the street and two from its right, that he even bothered to raise his own weaponry and begin to fire back.

Then he stopped as once again the sky lit up.

The wind which was swirling all about them as the storm began to impress itself on the already crippled town seemed to kick up dust between all the gun-toting men.

Hickok stood in all his majesty holding his famed pearl-handled pistols as his long mane of hair whipped the air itself.

Even Tom Dix had never seen such a sight as he paused beside a wooden upright, trying to judge where his targets actually were.

Wild Bill stood defiantly cocking his gun-hammers with his thumbs and squeezing his triggers as bullets tore through the lining of his frock-coat tails. Every shot which bore down on him seemed to pass within inches of his lean figure but none of them quite managed to hit him.

'He ain't human,' Black shouted out as the dust swirled between the marshal and himself, obscuring his target.

Hickok's poker face remained unchanged as Black made a break from the cover of the saloon and rushed towards the tall flamboyant figure, firing with every stride he took.

Firing twice as he dashed at the marshal he stumbled and fell at the tall man's feet. There was a long pause as Hickok continued firing over his terrified head.

'Start running, mister,' Hickok said through gritted teeth down at the sprawled Black.

Black quickly rose to his feet and raised both his pistols. A volley of shots rang out from Tom Dix's guns and felled the outlaw.

Hickok's fingers pulled the triggers again and they fell on empty chambers. Without even bothering to try and take cover, the tall marshal began to empty the spent shells from their chambers and start to reload his pair of deadly guns.

Grainger, seeing what had just happened, moved from the store doorway where he had been hiding. He knew the lawman was unable to return fire. Raising his gun he aimed at Hickok from the edge of the boardwalk.

'No you don't,' yelled Dan Shaw as he ran down the long wooden walkway towards the ruthless killer.

Grainger turned and fired quickly.

Dan suddenly felt the heat of the bullet as it caught him in his side. With every step he felt himself weaken until he finally stumbled and crashed into the ground.

Before the laughing Grainger had time to cock his hammer again he too felt the heat of hot lead as it passed through his body. Staggering backwards, he raised his hand and watched in horror as his pistol dropped from his paralysed fingers. Then he looked up and saw Tom Dix firing again from across the dark street.

It was the last thing he would ever see as he fell backwards through the glass window of a storefront. The falling daggers of glass finished the job Tom Dix's bullets had started.

Wild Bill Hickok pulled the hammers back again on both his reloaded guns and stepped over the dead figure of Black.

Then, with his cigar gripped between his teeth, McQueen fired wildly and fled down an alley.

Tom Dix leapt from the boardwalk and chased after the running McQueen. A bullet came down the narrow passageway between the two buildings and tore the Stetson off his head but he continued to pursue the last remaining outlaw.

Dix was now angrier than he had ever been in his entire life as the image of Dan Shaw being felled by one of the gang's bullets filled his thoughts.

Now he was going to kill the last of the dry-gulchers.

Reaching the end of the alley, Dix paused and stared into the darkness as a bullet tore a chunk of wood from the wall above his head. A thousand splinters showered over his hair. Dix fired back but knew his shot had gone astray.

The sky was still grumbling as Dix began to

walk forward into the shadows. Another bullet came from nowhere and tore at his left coat-sleeve, causing him to drop on to one knee as he felt the stinging of blood seeping from his wound.

'Quit now and I'll not kill you,' Dix called out into the shadows.

There was no response. McQueen was not about to give his hiding-place away by calling out any sort of reply.

Licking his dry lips, Dix began to rise when another bullet passed within inches of his face. He could feel the heat of the bullet on his skin.

No matter how hard he tried, he could not see where McQueen was. As he began to move again, the ground before him was hit by another bullet. Dust hit him in his face causing him to roll over onto his left side. As Dix lay there he could feel his blood soaking through his sleeve into the ground beneath him.

Then, as Dix held on to the Colt in his right hand, he saw a red glowing amid the darkness twenty feet away from here he lay.

Without a second's hesitation, Dix squeezed his trigger and heard the groaning as his bullet found its mark. It was a startled McQueen who staggered out of the gloom towards him. The shocked outlaw continued walking long after he had dropped his guns. As the sky lit up again, Dix could see the grim-faced outlaw walking, with a large hole in his blood-soaked shirt, as if unable to accept his own death. McQueen stopped a mere ten feet away from the rising Tom Dix.

As the glowing cigar fell from his lips he coughed and fell straight onto his face.

Dix stood for a few seconds staring down onto the body before turning and making his way back down the alley, clutching his arm as he went.

As the gunfighter staggered out into the wide street he saw Hickok holstering his weapons.

Reaching the side of the marshal he stopped.

'I got him, Bill.'

Hickok nodded and began to walk hurriedly past the body of Grainger to where Dan Shaw lay in a pool of blood.

'Is he OK, Bill?' Dix asked as he rested himself against a hitching pole and stared down at his pal.

Hickok knelt down and turned Dan over to lie face upward.

'Is it over, Wild Bill?' Dan asked as the marshal leaned over him.

'It's over, Dan,' Hickok replied.

'Is Dixie all right?'

Tom Dix stepped towards the pair clutching his arm. The injury burned like fire as its scarlet liquid ran down inside his coat-sleeve.

'I got myself winged, Dan,' Dix admitted.

James Butler Hickok helped Dan Shaw up on to his feet before staring at the two men who had once again shown that their courage had no limitations.

'I reckon I got a flesh wound, Dixie,' Dan said with a wince.

Tom Dix looked at the marshal. 'You scared the hell out of me, Bill. Walking down the street drawing their fire like that. Why did you do it?'

Hickok frowned. 'Someone had to lure the rats out of their holes, Dix.'

'Them *hombres* might have killed you,' Dan said as he peeled his bloodstained shirt away from his side to check his wound.

'It was a big gamble, Wild Bill,' Dix added.

'Everything in life is a gamble, boys,' Hickok said. 'And I'm the best gambler those varmints ever met.'

Suddenly the three men felt the cool spots of rain hitting their faces as the storm clouds at last began to yield and allow their precious bounty to fall over the town. Too late for the gang of outlaws.

Hickok ran his fingers through his mane of damp hair and grinned broadly as he began to head towards the saloon where the light still burned up in the second-floor window.

'You boys fix up them wounds,' Hickok told his pals.

'Where you going, Bill?' Dix asked.

'Somebody has to try and find all that money, Dix.'

FINALE

James Butler Hickok walked out of his hotel and adjusted the sleeves of his new frock-coat before taking a thin cigar and placing it between his teeth. He struck a match with his thumbnail, lifted the flame to its tip and puffed as he watched the two riders heading towards him.

Dix and Shaw greeted the imposing figure by touching the brims of their Stetsons.

'You boys going someplace?' Hickok asked as Tom Dix and Dan Shaw reined in their mounts directly below the boardwalk.

Tom Dix still had his arm in a sling whilst Dan's middle had remained tightly strapped since the heroic battle a few weeks earlier.

'Me and Dixie were thinking of heading west, Wild Bill,' Dan replied.

Hickok stepped to the edge of the boardwalk

and looked at the two figures atop their gelded mounts.

'West? What you want to head out there for?'

Dan looked wistfully at the marshal. 'I figure we might just find us a place where our kind might still fit in, Bill.'

'Besides, it ain't much fun staying in the same place for too long,' Dix added as he watched Hickok staring out at the array of saloons and gambling halls which stretched off down Abilene's long Main Street.

'I was getting itchy feet myself,' Hickok admitted as he stepped down and walked between the two horses which began to follow him towards the Drover's Rest Saloon.

As the two riders trailed the marshal they wondered how such a figure had managed to survive for so long with his total inability ever to shy away from trouble.

'Where would you go, Bill?' Dix asked.

Hickok mounted the boardwalk outside the saloon and paused as he began to think.

'There are plenty of towns were someone like me would fit in real easy, boys,' Hickok answered, as he turned to look at his two friends. 'I heard tell of a town called Deadwood. Sounds kind of ripe for a gambler like me.'

Dix looked hard at the tall figure.

'Guess the reward money was sure generous.'

Hickok flicked the ash from his cigar. 'Just another stake for another card game, Dix.'

'We're hanging on to our share, Bill. It might make things a tad easier in the future.' Dan smiled as he watched the lean man walking to the saloon and resting a hand on top of the swing doors.

'Future?' Hickok repeated the word as if it meant nothing to him. 'Sometimes the next card game is as much future as you're going to get.'

'How are your eyes, Wild Bill?' Dix asked quietly so that his words could only be heard by the man himself.

'Holding up, holding up,' Hickok replied.

Tom Dix began to turn his mount when he heard Hickok's voice again.

'You saved my bacon again back there in Spring City, Tom Dix. Thanks.'

Staring over his shoulder Dix smiled. 'Any time, James Butler. Any time.'

'So long, Bill,' Dan said as he aimed his black gelding after his friend's mount.

'We'll have to do this again some time,' Dix called out.

'Yep. Some time real soon.' Hickok pushed the swing doors apart and headed into the saloon without saying another word to the pair of riders as they rode out towards the blistering sun.

They sure had vinegar, Hickok thought.

The West was calling out to the two riders. They would not refuse to answer that call, as long as they had breath in their bodies and courage in their hearts.